ALSO BY

Gay Amish Romance Series

A Forbidden Rumspringa
A Clean Break
A Way Home

Contemporary
Valor on the Move
Cold War
Holding the Edge
Where the Lovelight Gleams
The Chimera Affair
The Argentine Seduction
Eight Nights
Daybreak
Love Match
City of Lights
Synchronicity

Historical
The Station
Semper Fi

Paranormal
Kick at the Darkness
A Taste of Midnight (free read!)

Fairy Tales
Rise

If
Only
In My
Dreams

Keira Andrews

An Original Publication From Keira Andrews

IF ONLY IN MY DREAMS
Written and published by Keira Andrews
Cover by Dar Albert
Formatted by Frostbite Publishing
Copyright © 2015 by Keira Andrews
All rights reserved.

First Paperback Edition, 2015

ISBN: 978-0-9940924-7-2

Thanks as always to Anne-Marie, Becky, Mary and Rachel for your invaluable beta reading and friendship.

This one's for all the readers who love holiday romances as much as I do. May your Christmas, Hanukkah, Kwanza, Solstice or Festivus be merry and bright!

Keira

One

Charlie

December 21ˢᵗ

"It's an act of God."

I forced a smile at the older woman behind the Sojourn Airways counter. "It's probably not the time for a theological debate, but I'd say it's more an act of Mother Nature." I tried to laugh, and it limped out as a sad little *ha-ha*.

Her flat expression, pulled tight by her graying bun, didn't so much as flicker. On her purple uniform vest was pinned a button that read: *Customer service is our bag. No baggage service fees!* "Sir, that's the official airline designation for weather conditions that are beyond our control."

"Right, gotcha. Look—" I checked her name tag. "Look, Susan, the thing is that I need to get on a flight to New York ASAP. JFK, LaGuardia, Newark—whichever. I'll even take Philly if I have to." I forced another smile. "I can always go for a cheesesteak."

The grim line of Susan's mouth was unchanging. "There are no flights in or out of SFO today. As I told you earlier, our system has already rebooked you."

"For the twenty-sixth!"

"Yes."

"But Christmas is the twenty-fifth!" The desperation I'd been trying to keep at bay with incredibly lame humor sank its claws into me with a mighty swipe.

"Is it? I had no idea."

Well, at the very least it seemed Susan's alien leaders had implanted a sarcasm chip even if they overlooked the compassion one. I inhaled deeply. "I realize this end-of-days-style fog has backed everything up, but you can't rebook me for *after Christmas*! That's ridiculous!" I thought of Ava's round little face, streaked with tears as I'd left for college, and how I'd promised I'd be home for the holidays. "I have plans. I have to get on the next flight out. I *have* to."

Susan tapped her computer, not even bothering to look at me now. "I didn't rebook you, Mr. Yates. The airline did. All flights yesterday were canceled as well, and this is the busiest travel season." She recited the lines in much the same manner as my mom reading out IKEA instructions as we put together the Billy bookshelf in my bedroom. "There are thousands and thousands of passengers ahead of you. The blizzard on the Eastern Seaboard had already contributed to a huge backlog before this fog set in."

"But I promised my baby sister I'd be home." I knew I was whining, and my voice wavered as my throat tightened.

Susan's mouth turned down as she glanced at me. Her tone softened. "If there was anything I could do, I would do it."

This unexpected sympathy made it worse somehow. I cleared my throat, the threat of imminent tears a horrifying possibility. *Don't do it, Charlie. Man up.* "Okay. Thank you. Do you think I could get out on another airline?"

"I'm afraid they're all in the same boat."

"Standby?"

She shook her head and waved a hand at the mass of humanity clogging the terminal behind me. "Everyone has the same idea. As I mentioned, there were already dozens of flights canceled before yours. The twenty-sixth is the absolute earliest you'll be able to get out, and that's assuming this fog lifts soon and the rain stops. And if it doesn't start snowing heavily on the East Coast again."

With a nod, I shuffled away from the counter, dragging my huge, stupidly pink suitcase behind me. I might be a total homo and unashamed of it, but fuchsia was not a color I'd have chosen for my luggage. Ava had picked it with such delight that I hadn't been able to say no. At least it had four wheels and was expandable, which was handy since it was stuffed with Christmas gifts.

I'd gotten Ava some old-school Transformers building sets and retro *Star Wars* action figures I'd hunted down. Princess Leia was her favorite, since even at eight, Ava had excellent taste and understood that the classic trilogy was superior like whoa. On eBay, I'd found Hoth Leia, original recipe double-bun Leia, and even a rare Cloud City Leia, along with a bad-ass Boba Fett.

Now Ava wouldn't get any of it for Christmas morning. I wouldn't be able to wake up with her at the ass-crack of dawn to open our stockings, then burst into our parents' room to drag them out of bed because Christmas was way too much fun for sleeping.

A preteen standing by a pile of luggage whined, "It's not *fair!*" to her parents, her arms crossed over her chest and tears in her eyes.

Snorting, I muttered, "Since when has life been fair?" Pretty freaking rarely in my estimation, and never when it came to Ava. I escaped into the nearest bathroom to splash water on my face and get my shit together. My cheeks puffed as I blew out a long breath and examined a fabulous new red spot on my chin in the mirror.

I'd gotten a haircut yesterday since my Aunt Wendy was going to do a group portrait for us by the tree with her fancy camera. This was a big Christmas for the Yates family, and now I wasn't going to be there. I ran a hand over my thin brown hair, which curled at the ends if I didn't keep it short. Ava's did too, but it wasn't quite long enough yet to curl fully.

We'd Skyped the other night, and she'd proudly run a brush through her couple inches of growing hair. She'd gained weight too, and I couldn't wait to hold her and feel her solid and healthy in my arms.

I had to suck in a breath, the ache to see her and my parents again a hollow burn in my chest. I grimaced at my reflection. My eyes were already red from the prior night's insomnia. I never slept well the night before taking a flight due to my paranoia that I'd miss my alarm somehow.

Ava and I had the same eyes: a deep, warm blue, easily bloodshot, and not good at hiding emotions. Our grandpa always said that even though we were ten years apart, we should have been twins.

I'm actually going to miss Christmas. I'm going to break my promise.

The fear that I'd been trying to keep at bay roared up, and I squeezed my eyes shut. I knew it had only been a dream, and that dreams weren't prophecies or visions, or any of that shit. Yet I shuddered as I remembered the dream hospital I'd finally been able to reach after missing Christmas because I'd kept driving down the wrong roads, taking endless turns.

The dream—*nightmare*—doctor had said the relapse had happened too quickly, and there was nothing they could have done. My parents had already left because Ava was gone. I was too late. My baby sister was dead and I hadn't been able to say goodbye.

Choking down a swell of nausea, I closed my eyes and breathed in and out.

It was only a dream. She's okay.

I splashed my face again, getting water all over my hoodie and not caring. Of course they were out of paper towels, so I wiped my hands on my jeans.

I aimlessly walked the terminal, squeezing between clumps of fellow dispirited would-be passengers and their mounds of baggage.

My messenger bag tugged at my neck, and I impatiently adjusted it on my shoulder. It was Saturday morning, and school was out for kids, exams were over for college, and winter vacation was here. Too bad we'd apparently be spending it at San Francisco International Airport, or for me, back in my empty dorm.

Fa la la la la.

A bank of TVs blasted CNN, and I stopped to watch the anchor with suspiciously gleaming teeth put on his serious face beneath a swoop of perfectly coiffed hair. Pulsing red letters took up half the screen, screaming: *WEATHER ALERT!*

"We've just survived snowmageddon in the east, and now it's the West Coast's turn! Torrential rain has hit the Pacific Northwest, extending down into Northern California. And it's *FOGmageddon* for San Francisco!"

I rolled my eyes. The media's impulse to add "-mageddon" to otherwise non-threatening words needed to be taken out back and shot, along with "gate" suffixes. Watergate was a million years ago. Get over it, people.

The smug bastard on TV actually smiled. His name was probably Chip, or perhaps Blaine. "Along with the rain, the fog in San Francisco has reduced visibility to the extent that officials are advising folks to *stay home*. Forget pea soup—this stuff is molasses!"

With a sigh, I trudged on. Might as well catch the AirTrain to the BART station. The thought of hauling ass—and my giant suitcase— back to a ghost town campus was seriously depressing. I reminded myself this wouldn't be the worst Christmas I'd ever had, but it was cold comfort. The last two yuletides jointly held that title, and I prayed they would never be defeated.

I found the AirTrain sign, along with another: *Rental Car Center*. I stopped in my tracks, barely avoiding getting rear-ended by a luggage cart and a man who muttered a curse as he wheeled around me. I called out an apology as I stared at the sign, my pulse increasing with a hum through my veins.

Was it possible? Could I make it back in time if I drove? There was rain and fog here and snow out there, but surely in the middle I could make up some time? If I powered through on Red Bull and Twizzlers, I could do it.

Yanking out my phone, I googled the driving time from San Francisco to Norwalk, Connecticut.

43 h (2,952.6 mi) via I-80 E

It was basically straight across the country through Nevada, Utah, Wyoming, Nebraska, Iowa, Illinois, Indiana, Ohio, Pennsylvania, New Jersey, New York, and finally into Connecticut. Which sounded insanely exhausting, but was totally doable. Factoring in stops for eating and a few hours of sleep in the backseat here and there, I'd get there with time to spare. I could make it home for Christmas morning.

Adrenaline zinged through me with this new plan of action, and I hurried to the AirTrain platform. The loop through the terminals to the Car Rental Center was interminable, and I drummed my fingers on the plastic handle of my suitcase until the woman crammed between me and the door gave me an understandable death glare.

I practically dove down the concourse, dragging my suitcase along. Amazingly enough, there were hardly any people at all in the rental area, and I grinned as I approached the first counter. I wouldn't even have to wait! This was clearly an amazing plan, and perhaps even an Act of God. It was meant to be.

NO VEHICLES AVAILABLE

I blinked at the sign. Okay, next counter. My heart sank a little when I saw a sold-out sign there too. Onto the next. And the next.

And the next.

Of course there were no lines. There were no damn cars left. I kept going just in case, but each rental company I passed was out of vehicles.

As I approached the last one—one of those cheap car places stuck in the back corner—my feet dragged and my shoulders slumped. For all of fifteen minutes, I'd thought Christmas and my promise to my sister could be saved.

As I neared Expedition Car Rental, my heart skipped a beat. I peered closer, scanning the area. There was no sign. There was no sign! In a burst of excitement I raced the rest of the way, barreling into the counter. The young woman behind it jerked her head up from her computer.

"Hi! Sorry to startle you. I need a car. Do you have a car?" I forced myself to take a calming breath and read her name tag. "Sorry, Sook-Yin. I really need a car." I smiled what I hoped was my most charming smile, because I didn't need Sook-Yin refusing my patronage on suspicion of me being on crack or meth or huffing the nitrous oxide from whipped cream bottles.

She tilted her head and gave me a regretful closed-lip smile. "I'm so sorry. I just rented our last vehicle."

Panic and disappointment combined to make my mouth dry and chest tight. "Please. You have to have another one. I'm begging you. I will get down on my knees. I'll pay extra. I'll pay whatever you want. *Please*. I need a car. Or truck. SUV. Minivan. Motorcycle. Anything with wheels and an engine."

"I'm very sorry."

I dropped my head to the counter with a dull *thunk*. "I can't believe this is happening. Please let me wake up in my dorm and realize this nightmare was just my subconscious being a bag of dicks as usual."

Sook-Yin made a sound that might have been a stifled laugh, but her tone was sympathetic. "I really am sorry. Hold on, let me check our other area locations. You might get lucky."

Other locations! I hadn't even thought of that. I lifted my head and watched her type, holding my breath. *Please, please, please, please…*

She sighed and tucked her dark hair behind her ear. "Nope. But I'll check the other companies for you."

My lungs burned as I waited, my hands in fists to stop from drumming my fingers on the counter. The CIA should forget waterboarding—watching someone else search for information on a computer when you're dying to know the answer is pure torture. Sook-Yin tapped, her eyes scanning the screen, and my heart pounded. There had to be one freaking car left to rent in the Bay Area. There had to be. I'd go to Oakland. Jesus, I'd bus it to Modesto if I had to. *Please, please, please, please…*

Then she gave me the head tilt/sad smile again, and I knew it was hopeless. She didn't have to say it. I tried to smile back. "Thanks for checking. It was really nice of you." My brain whirled. What about Greyhound? Sure, it was the busiest travel time of the year and the buses would be loaded with people who couldn't get flights, but maybe. "I guess I'll try the bus."

She winced. "I've heard they're overbooked. And there was that mechanic's strike? There aren't enough buses, apparently."

"I guess the trains are sold out too."

"Do you want me to check?" Her gaze shifted to something behind me, and she smiled. "Excuse me for a second. Ah, there you are," she said to someone. "Did you find the Starbucks?"

"Yes, thank you. I'm caffeinated and ready to hit the road."

My whole body seized. It couldn't be. It was not possible. *Not. Possible.*

I slowly turned and…wow. Gavin Bloomberg—still as annoyingly tall and hot as ever—was actually standing there in a fitted brown leather jacket with a blue travel mug in one hand and a little rolling gray suitcase resting by his suede Pumas. He blinked at me, and after a moment his lip curled.

"Charlie?" He appeared as horrified as I felt.

Of all the car rental places in all the freaking world… I concentrated on a civil tone. After all, we were eighteen and officially adults now. "Gavin."

"Uh…hi." He stared at me the way he might a piece of gum after walking around on it all day and prying it free from the bottom of his shoe, with little pebbles and a bunch of shit dried into it. He ran a hand through his thick, short hair, and even under dull fluorescents I couldn't help but notice the rich auburn highlights. His sideburns were longer than when I'd last seen him at graduation in June.

I was weirdly struck by a memory of the summer we'd met, and how almost every day we'd stretch out in the sun by the pond, and he'd close his eyes while I watched his hair dry, the whole time aching to touch.

"Do you guys know each other?" Sook-Yin asked.

I nodded. "I guess. Not really. I mean, we went to high school together." This was definitely a nightmare, but sadly I was all too awake. Time to evacuate. "Well, I should go."

"Wait!" Sook-Yin's face lit up. "Are you both trying to get to the same place? Maybe you could drive together?"

My brain was so dumbfounded at Gavin's unexpected presence that I hadn't even processed that he'd obviously rented a vehicle. Oh. My. God. Of *course* he'd snagged the last car. Of course. Because he got everything he wanted.

Gavin glanced between me and Sook-Yin. "I'm going back to Norwalk."

"Me too. But we can't..." I waved a hand between us.

Sook-Yin's brow creased. "But it's the perfect solution, isn't it? I can add another driver to the contract. I'll even waive the extra fee. You're already paying more since you're under twenty-five. Obviously it's up to you, though."

"Uh..." Gavin stared at her with dawning horror in his brown eyes.

I shared that horror. There was no way—no effing way!—Gavin Bloomberg and I could drive to Connecticut together. It was impossible. It was unthinkable. It was the worst idea ever.

But fuck me. It was my shot.

As much as I hated it, this was my way home for Christmas. Gavin and I could split the driving and gas, and we could totally make it for the twenty-fifth with tons of time to spare.

"I can't...it's..." Clutching his travel mug, Gavin stared at me.

"I promised Ava I'd be home for Christmas."

The hard edges of Gavin's gaze softened, and he exhaled. After a long moment, he nodded. "Then I guess we'd better get going."

"I'm so glad this worked out. What a small world. Can you give me your license?" Sook-Yin started entering my info, apparently oblivious to the tension in the air. "Wait, do you two actually live on the same street?"

Gavin and I nodded silently.

"Wow, what are the odds?" Smiling, she printed off a new contract. "Do you go to the same school out here too?"

"No. He's at USF and I'm at Stanford," Gavin answered.

I blinked. He knew where I went? Mom's voice echoed in my mind.

"Hon, guess who's going to Frisco for college too?"

"Please don't call it Frisco." I rolled another T-shirt and squeezed it into *my pink suitcase. "And no, who?"*

"Your friend Gavin! Isn't that wonderful? I'm so glad you'll have someone from home out there with you."

The fact that Gavin was most certainly not my friend—and had not been my friend since Pete Stiffler's party at the beginning of ninth grade—had been lost on my mom. In her defense, her plate had been pretty fucking full the last few years, and I'd never even hinted at a problem.

"I just need you both to sign here, and initial here, here, and here." Sook-Yin circled spots on the contract.

Gavin picked up the pen, passing it to me when he was finished. The plastic was warm from his fingers, and my stomach danced the way it used to when Gavin was close by. I felt fourteen again and hopelessly out of my depth.

After marking my last initial, I passed the contract back to Sook-Yin, who ripped off a copy and slid it into a narrow folder. She handed Gavin a key. "Here you go. It's in spot C-thirty-seven, but since it's the last car left, it won't be hard to find. It's a Jetta, but don't worry, I only charged you economy class. Have a safe drive, and happy holidays!"

We smiled and thanked her, and I followed Gavin to the garage. In silence, we rode the elevator down, and in the subterranean concrete maze, the only sound was the rumbling drone of our suitcase wheels and the odd car driving by. The Jetta waited, navy blue and four-doored, boxy with its sedate and practical German engineering.

A man chewing gum approached from the little Expedition office, which was more like a shack. He wore coveralls and a baseball cap. "Got the last one, huh?"

I smiled tightly. "Yep."

We inspected the car, circling it to make sure there were no dings or scratches. Gavin signed the form, and the guy started the engine. "Tank is full, and you're ready to go. Have a good one." He shuffled off.

Gavin popped the trunk and eyed my pink monstrosity. "Are you moving back or something?"

"No." I stubbornly didn't explain further and hefted up the suitcase.

After fitting in his little gray case, Gavin closed the trunk. "I guess I'll drive first?"

"Sure." It was all very civil and *so freaking bizarre,* oh my God.

I went around to the passenger side, buckling my belt and pushing the seat back for maximum leg room. I was only five-nine compared to Gavin's ridiculous six-one, but I still liked to stretch out. Especially since we were going to be in this car for forty-three hours—and that was with clear weather and no traffic jams. I barely resisted the urge to whimper. Just getting out of the Bay Area took forever in good conditions, let alone *FOGmageddon.*

After adjusting the mirrors, Gavin backed up. Neither of us spoke as he navigated the winding levels of the garage, and at the exit he stuck the provided parking ticket into the machine. The mechanical arm jerked up to let us pass, and home had never felt so incredibly far away.

Two

Gavin

Charlie Yates was actually sitting beside me in the rental car. I'd had some surreal moments in my life—also involving Charlie Yates, come to think of it—but this one had to take the cake and the freaking cherry on top. I'd checked the car rentals on a whim, not wanting to go back to my dorm and twiddle my thumbs while I waited days for another flight. Now here I was with…*him*. Of all people.

"I could have walked faster than this," he grumbled. It was the first thing he'd said in miles.

I snapped, "And it's my fault two lanes are blocked up ahead? I'd go faster if I could." The sun was distressingly low in the sky, and we were barely in Sacramento.

He stared at the minivan ahead of us. "I didn't say it was your fault. I'm saying it took us three hours just to get out of the city, and now we're crawling slower than I walk."

"At least there's no fog here. And the rain is lessening."

He apparently couldn't argue with that, although I bet he wanted to. Instead he shrugged. "True." He scoffed. "I hate those dumb

IF ONLY IN MY DREAMS

decals. *Baby on board.* Right, because *now* people won't hit you when they totally would have before."

"I guess they figure better safe than sorry." As the radio blared a commercial, I pressed the scan button.

"I just wish the universe would give us a freaking break already. I mean, really? A truck had to jackknife and spill its gravel over two lanes?"

"It could be worse. I hope no one was injured."

Charlie shot me a glare. "Obviously I also hope no one was hurt, Saint Gavin."

My stomach did a weird little twist. I hadn't heard the nickname in so long, but now it was thorny with derision instead of the laughing tease that had accompanied it under the hazy August sun to the song of cicadas.

As we crawled along, I eyed the yellow baby sticker on the minivan—it really was stupid—and tried not to hum along to the new Taylor Swift song. I could only imagine the crap Charlie would give me for that. He probably listened to cool indie bands that pressed their own LPs and didn't believe in iTunes.

"Hanukkah is late this year, huh?"

I blinked in surprise that he knew. Which was silly, because it was on the calendar, so why shouldn't he have noticed? "Yeah. But it's never been a big deal in my family. We're not very good Jews. My parents are in Jamaica anyway."

I kept my eyes on the road, but could feel his assessing gaze. "They're not going to be in Norwalk?"

"Nope." I worked on a casual tone, as if everything was totally normal with my folks. On paper, it was. They'd be home for New Year's Eve, and they did invite me to Jamaica—I was the one who said I wanted to go skiing instead. Although as soon as they found out Candace was involved, they couldn't endorse it fast enough.

And that was exactly why I hadn't wanted to go to the resort. There would be so much time to *talk*, and even if I finally had the guts to say it, I knew they wouldn't want to hear it.

"You're not meeting them down there?"

The traffic had sped up to twenty whole miles an hour, and I pressed gently on the gas. "Nah."

"Then why are you going home?"

"I'm going skiing in Vermont with Candace and her family."

"Right, of course. *Candace*." He drawled her name in a sing-songy way that had me gripping the steering wheel.

"Yes. Candace." He muttered something under his breath, and I snapped off the radio, protective anger surging up. "What was that?"

"Nothing." Charlie flipped the radio back on and jumped from station to station.

Man, he had some nerve. As if he had any right to say a thing about Candace after what he'd done. I thought of the tinny dance music and crowded tables of the pizzeria that night in junior year, the smell of grease in the air and blood dripping on the white tiles.

I opened my mouth to tell him that Candace was an amazing person and I wasn't going to put up with a single insult about her. And besides that, she and I were only friends now. But no. Forget it. I didn't have to justify anything to Charlie Yates.

I didn't owe him any explanations. Not anymore. Not after what he'd said and done.

The more I thought about it, the more I wanted to pull over and kick his butt out. This was *my* rental car. It was on my credit card. Why had I given in? Ugh, this was the *worst*. I wanted to sing pop songs at the top of my lungs and stop at cheesy roadside attractions—the World's Biggest Random Whatever. But Charlie would undoubtedly roll his eyes and grumble and basically make it no fun at all. When we'd first met, Charlie had been the most fun person I'd ever met. But that was a long time ago.

His phone buzzed, and I couldn't help but listen to his half of the conversation as I turned down the radio so he could hear.

"Hey, Mom. Yeah. We're fine. I know, crazy coincidence. Ha, yeah, a Christmas miracle." He was silent for a few moments. "It's slow going. Hopefully it'll clear up soon." Charlie tapped his fingers on the heel of his sneaker where his ankle was crossed over his other leg. "Uh-huh. He's good. He says hi."

I cleared my throat and called, "Hi, Mrs. Yates." I hadn't talked to her in years, but she'd always waved if she drove by me on our street.

"We will. *Yes*, Mom. We're not twelve. Wait, she is? Of course." When he spoke again, his voice was suddenly gentle and *sweet* in a way I'd forgotten Charlie could be. "Hey, Bear. How was today? Did you go to Madison's party?" He listened, hunched over toward the window. "Yeah, I'm on my way. I'm doing everything I can to beat Santa there, okay? I promise."

Right.

Here was the reason I couldn't pull over and tell Charlie Yates to find another way home to Connecticut. Ava had only been six when she was diagnosed. I could still remember the way Candace's eyes had glistened for a little girl she'd never met as she'd whispered, *"They say it's leukemia. Isn't that terrible?"* And it had been. Awful and unfair, and I'd wanted so badly to go down the block and knock on the door to tell them how sorry I was. Tell Charlie how sorry I was.

For everything.

As he gently teased his little sister on the phone and listened like every word she said was the most important he'd ever heard, memories flashed through my mind of the first time I'd seen Charlie.

It was the summer I moved to Norwalk after eighth grade. My parents were at work, and I was moping around my bedroom. I'd heard Ava's joyful shriek first, and had pressed my nose against the glass of the window. As I watched, a gangly boy piggybacking a little girl had raced past my new house on Tremont Street like a bat out of hell, a burst of fearless abandon.

They'd been gone in a flash, leaving the serene, tree-lined street quiet again but for the muffled drone of a lawn mower under the blazing July sun. I stood there at the window for another minute, hoping. Then I'd heard Ava's ecstatic shout again. I'd watched as

Charlie had zoomed by a second time, Ava bouncing wildly on his back.

I'd realized they were circling the block, and on the next pass, I stood on my lawn, not even pretending to be doing anything but waiting for them. Charlie had slowed when he spotted my awkward wave.

"Hey! You're new."

"Um, hey. Yeah. I'm Gavin. We just moved here from Long Island."

"Want to go swimming?"

It had been as easy as that.

"Well, did you tell Madison that you wanted to play with Whitney too?"

I smiled to myself. It was nice to hear that Ava was embroiled in eight-year-old schoolyard-type politics. It was so…normal. I'd glimpsed her once in a while, but the last time I'd really seen her had been more than a year ago.

My throat tightened at the memory—Charlie piggybacking her around the block like he used to, this time on a fall day with crunchy leaves underfoot and a heavy gray sky that seemed ready to collapse with impending rain.

It had been chance that I'd passed the window and saw them. Ava hadn't shrieked this time, and Charlie walked carefully, no reckless flight with sneakers slapping the pavement. Ava's cheek had rested on his shoulder, and her bald head was too pale. Even though she'd been seven, in a way she'd seemed even smaller than she had when I first met them.

I'd pressed my nose against the glass as they went by, too much of a coward to go out and say hi. I'd assured myself I was perfectly justified after the pizzeria incident, but had still waited to see them pass again. The sidewalk had remained empty but for Mr. Garrison walking his black lab.

"Okay. Love you too, Bear. Give me a growl." Charlie laughed softly and scratched behind his ear, and a rush of nostalgia flowed through me. He had a chicken pox scar back there that he'd said still itched after years.

From the corner of my eye, I watched his long fingers on his neck, wondering what they'd feel like touching me now that we were grown up. His jaw was more prominent, his full lips a red that was positively…the only word that came to mind was *juicy*.

Stop. Stop right now. He would never want me again. I blew my chance. Besides, I don't want a jerk like him.

As he hung up, I stared straight ahead, trying and undoubtedly failing to pretend I hadn't been listening. It was pointless, so I cleared my throat. "How is she?"

Charlie was silent so long I thought he wouldn't answer. "In remission. For now, at least. She's still weak, but getting stronger."

"I really hope she'll be okay. I'm sure she will be. She's tough."

He shrugged and tapped at his phone, the careless tone back. "Yeah. I guess we'll see. I need to piss. Want to stop soon?"

"Sure. I think there's a McDonald's coming up."

"Cool." His phone buzzed, and he laughed softly as he read the message. The question hovered on the tip of my tongue before I swallowed it roughly. *Is that* him? *Is he still your boyfriend?*

Did you ever think of me?

I'd only ever seen the boyfriend once. Beginning of junior year, before that night at the pizzeria made everything worse. As Charlie's thumbs flew and he texted whoever it was back, traffic crept to a near standstill. We inched along, and the memory stubbornly filled my mind.

Brad and Paul were talking about the football game, but their grumbling washed over me in a series of grunts as I watched Charlie hurrying down the steps toward the curb, his head low like usual. A Jeep with the top down waited. The blond guy behind the wheel looked like a senior, but I didn't recognize him.

When he spotted Charlie, the guy smiled brightly and lifted his chin. He tapped the steering wheel, keeping time with the beat of a song I couldn't hear. I couldn't see Charlie's expression as he climbed in, but then he tilted his head and they kissed.

26

They actually honest-to-God kissed, right there by the curb. Charlie kissed another guy. A guy who wasn't me. My lungs constricted, and I was going to explode or pass out or maybe die.

"Earth to Gavin?"

I managed to suck in a rush of air as Candace linked her arm with mine and bumped our shoulders together. It shouldn't have hurt, seeing Charlie with that guy. I shouldn't have cared. But wow. Charlie was really gay. And he wasn't hiding it.

He wasn't a coward like me.

Candace must have followed my frozen gaze. "Oh, I guess that's his new boyfriend. Tim something. Nina said he goes to Jefferson."

I couldn't shove the words past my tight throat. Couldn't even nod. Charlie and his boyfriend were laughing about something as this Tim person put the Jeep in drive. I hadn't seen Charlie laugh in so long.

What did I expect? He sure didn't owe me anything. We didn't even know each other anymore. And I knew that was my fault, and the low hum of regret I lived with constantly crescendoed as my eyes burned. I bit the inside of my cheek so hard I tasted the metallic copper of blood.

Candace was still talking. "He's going through so much with his poor sister. I'm glad he found someone. And before you say it, shut up, Brad. Yes, I can read your tiny mind."

I watched them drive away, the Jeep joining the line of vehicles leaving school. I was inside out, my guts hanging there raw and bloody.

"Gav?" Candace elbowed me, and I managed to turn my head and focus on her frown. "What's wrong?" She screwed up her face. "You're not some secret homophobe, are you?"

"Of course not." My voice sounded alien to me, but Candace's brow smoothed out. "It's great for him. Really cool. Awesome."

And why shouldn't Charlie have a boyfriend? I should be glad, since the idea of him lonely hit me with a deep pang—even as the thought of Charlie and *Tim*—or someone new—sent jealousy boiling through me.

As we inched along the interstate, Charlie put his phone away in his pocket. He turned up the radio and hit the scan button, listening to each station for two seconds before continuing on, never seeming to find what he was looking for.

Charlie

I wasn't sure if it was the crick in my neck or the drool dripping down my chin that woke me. Inhaling sharply, I jolted up straight. It was dark, and I blinked at the red glow of taillights. Beside me, Gavin turned down the radio, which had been playing a bad cover of "Santa Baby." I rubbed my eyes. "Where are we?"

"We passed Wells, Nevada, a little while back."

The green display on the dashboard said it was just after eleven p.m. I pulled out my phone and read a text from Mom.

How's it going? You and Gavin be careful on those roads. Don't drive too fast. Christmas will be whenever you get here. Xxxxx

I tamped down the swell of emotion. Most people did "xoxo," but when I was little my mom always kissed my forehead, chin, both cheeks, and then the tip of my nose before I went to sleep. She did it with Ava too. I guess it's our family's thing, although my dad was always big on the bear hugs. He and Mom are kind of perfect that way. Yin and yang, Aunt Wendy says.

"Everything okay?"

I glanced at Gavin, who looked over with a concerned furrow between his brows. "Um, yeah."

I went back to my phone and opened my map. Why was Gavin being...*nice?* He hadn't deigned to pay me the slightest bit of attention in years—aside from that day in the pizza place, the thought of which sent a prickly rush of anger and shame through me. But earlier when he'd asked about Ava, he'd seemed sincere.

I shifted in my seat, uncrossing my legs. When I'd woken up that morning from my uneasy pre-airport sleep, I'd expected to be back home in Norwalk by now. But here I was in a car in Buttfuck, Nevada—with *Gavin Bloomberg*. It was so goddamned *weird*.

And as I focused on the map, I realized I was going to be in a car with Gavin for a long-ass time. "We're, like, six hours behind schedule. At least."

"Yeah, it sucks. It really took forever getting out of the Bay Area." He yawned widely.

With a stab of guilt, I realized he'd been driving since that morning. "I can drive now. Sorry, I didn't mean to pass out for so long."

"It's okay. Should probably get more gas too. At the next station we can switch. There's a town coming up."

"Cool." I fiddled with the laces on my sneaker. This part of the interstate had two lanes in each direction, and white headlights passed by on the other side of a grassy median. The land looked flat as a pancake, but it was too dark to see much. "You ever driven across the country before?"

"Nope. You?"

"No."

In the ensuing silence, broken only by that incredibly annoying Paul McCartney Christmas song on the radio, I stared out the window, trying to see beyond the flat scrub that disappeared into inky blackness. I racked my brain for something to say. That first summer, Gavin and I would talk for hours and hours about nothing. Comics and movies, and just…stuff. Now we could barely handle the kind of small talk you'd make in a taxi or on a plane.

"How's Tim?"

Whoa. I swiveled my head to gape at him. "What?"

"That's his name, isn't it? That guy you were seeing from Jefferson High?" Gavin adjusted one of the heating vents, casual as anything.

"Yeah. That's his name. I didn't…how did you know?"

He laughed uneasily. "What, you thought it was a secret or something? Everyone knew. It wasn't a big deal. It's not like you hid it."

"No one mentioned it to me." I wrapped one of my laces around my index finger, cutting off the circulation. It wasn't that I cared about people knowing I was gay—he was right, I hadn't hidden it. But the idea of Gavin actually talking about me and Tim (probably with *Candace*) torpedoed bile up my esophagus.

"Seemed like you never really talked to anyone at school the last couple years. You always had your earbuds in, and outside class you didn't join in anything."

"I was a little busy with my dying sister." I tugged the lace harder.

"Oh, I know. I'm not saying…you just seemed…"

"What?"

"Angry." He shrugged. "You intimidated people."

I released the lace and let the blood back into my fingertip. "So? I don't care what people think."

"I know. I always admired that about you. Most guys I knew in junior high wouldn't have spent so much time playing with their little sister. You never worried about being 'cool' or whatever."

The flush of pleasure that warmed me was beyond stupid and annoying. "Well, Tim was a cool guy, but we weren't serious. He's been at Penn State since last year. Having a good time from what I see on Facebook. Bagging a lot of hot guys."

"Oh yeah? Cool." Gavin cleared his throat. "What about you?"

How was this real life? Sure, just talking about banging guys with Gavin. NBD. "Sure, college has been fun. Plenty of guys to hook up with at USF. For a Jesuit school, the party scene is pretty wild." I'd fooled around with a few students, but that was it. Sex was fun, but I wasn't looking for a boyfriend.

"I was wondering about that. Not the party scene, but the religious thing. I didn't think you were a big believer?"

I laughed. "Oh, I'm not. But they take heathens too. I wrote an essay about how cancer kills faith, and they gave me a full ride. It would have been an in-state school for me if they hadn't. I guess they figure they can save my soul. But I haven't actually met any Bible thumpers. It's been chill."

"That's good. What's your major going to be?"

"No idea. I'm taking a bunch of stuff this year, and we'll see if anything sticks. What about you?"

"Engineering."

"Nice." I should have known he'd be doing something super smart. His dad was a civil engineer, and I still wasn't really sure what he actually did, but it was probably hard.

"How are your parents?" he asked.

"Good. Better now. It's been hard with Ava and everything."

"Yeah, I bet. Is your dad still at the same firm?"

I smiled briefly. "He just made partner, actually. It was a pretty big deal."

"Cool!" Gavin's face lit up, a grin pushing the dimples into his cheeks and making my stomach flip-flop like a fish on the bottom of a boat. *Do not go there, Charlie. Get a grip.* "Is your mom going back to work now?"

"Not sure. I think she's gotten her fill of hospitals, you know? But she might do some private nursing or something. We'll see." I cleared my throat and stared out the windshield at the red lights. "How are your folks?"

The bright-eyed remnants of his grin vanished, and Gavin sped up to change lanes and pass the car in front of us. "They're fine. Oh, there's the exit for that town." He accelerated more to get back in the right lane.

Huh. As we exited the interstate and pulled into a gas station, I rolled it around in my mind. Gavin and his parents had been tight, but maybe something had changed? Sure, Hanukkah might not be a super important high holy day or whatever, but it was totally weird that they'd spend the holidays without him. But maybe they'd wanted him to come and he'd elected to be with *Candace* instead.

Ugh. She of the perky tits and golden hair and even, gleaming white teeth. Just thinking about her made me clench my fists.

"Candace is making the new guy feel right at home!" Pete Stiffler crowed with a braying laugh.

I yanked open the car door and stalked into the gas station, shivering in the surprisingly cold night. Bells jingled merrily, and it looked like Santa's workshop had barfed all over the interior of the convenience store, with garlands and cheap ornaments strung over the shelves and lights along the tops of the fridges. The middle-aged guy behind the counter wore reindeer horns.

I nodded to him as I grabbed a Red Bull and a bunch of snacks, wondering what the Bloombergs thought of Miss Candace Allen. She'd been near the top of our class and was going to Columbia, because of course she had beauty *and* brains. It was nauseating.

As I surveyed the chip aisle, wondering if Gavin still loved sour cream and onion, I sighed. I knew I wasn't being fair. How could I blame Candace for seeing him at that stupid party and grabbing him? It wasn't her fault he wanted her back. Of course he did—she was a straight guy's perfect cheerleader fantasy.

Wasn't her fault he didn't want me.

Through the window, I could see him pumping the gas, watching the numbers climb. He'd been beautiful the first day I saw him, and he'd grown into a gorgeous man. Tall and lean and long legged, and…why the hell was I thinking about this? So what if he was good looking? I'd thought we were friends, but I'd been nothing to him. Some little experiment he'd tossed aside for the hetero delights of Candace Allen. I hadn't even been worth *talking* to after school started.

Jerking away from the window, I grabbed a bag of Doritos. After I paid the cashier, I climbed behind the wheel of the Jetta. When Gavin got in the passenger seat, he tucked away the gas receipt in the glove box.

He asked, "I guess we'll just take turns filling up? And at the end we'll see if one of us paid more."

"Sure," I gritted out as I started the engine. I could see him watching me from the corner of my eye as I peeled out of the station.

"What? Do you not want to do the gas that way?"

"The gas is fine. And obviously I owe you for half the car too. I'll pay you when we get home."

"I know you will. I'm not…okay. Fine." He flipped on the radio and left it on a station playing my mom's favorite carol.

"They looked up and saw a star.
Shining in the east beyond them far.
And to the earth it gave great light
And so it continued both day and night."

My breath stuttered as I remembered last Christmas and driving my mom home from the hospital after another of Ava's endless treatments. I couldn't sing for shit, but as we'd passed all the twinkling lights and snowmen, I'd warbled the verses I could remember.

It had only made my mom cry harder, but then she'd gripped my hand and said I was right—we couldn't give up hope. I'd only sung it to make her feel better because she liked it, but I guess it had been the right thing to do.

The star shining in the east now was the town of West Wendover. We drove into Utah over two faded white lines painted on the road, under the watchful eye of a giant neon cowboy and the glittering lure of casinos. A sign informed us we were now in mountain time, which made me feel like we'd just fallen another hour behind schedule.

Past the undaunted dazzle of buffets, country cover bands, slot machines, and Arby's, rocky hills rose. Soon we were cloaked in darkness again, with only a few fellow travelers on the road as midnight ticked by. As we went, the hills disappeared and the flat ground became strangely bright. "Jesus. Is it snowing?"

Gavin leaned forward in his seat, peering intently. "I don't think so, but I guess it snowed earlier? It's all white. Oh, wait—look at the sign."

Bonneville Salt Flats Recreation Area

I exhaled. Salt I could handle. We'd have enough snow to deal with as we went farther east. "Oh, duh. Wow. That's a lot of salt."

We passed the miles and miles of salt flats, the carols playing softly, people singing about joy to the world, decking the halls, and silent nights. After a while, I realized Gavin was asleep. His lips were parted, and his chest rose and fell evenly. He'd taken off his leather jacket and folded it against the window as a pillow.

His thick eyebrows had been pretty messy when we first met, but he'd started plucking in high school. The urge to reach over and run my finger over his left brow was ridiculous, and I ripped my gaze back to the road.

Unfortunately, the highway was a flat line in danger of hypnotizing me, so I let myself look again. Gavin wore a red Henley with three open buttons at the neck. Dark hair poked out from the collar, and I wondered how thick it was over his chest.

Turning my head, I forced in a long, deep breath and held it for a few seconds before exhaling. I wondered if his lips would still feel surprisingly soft, and if—

I took another breath and held it for longer this time as I clutched the wheel. What ifs would only make this trip even more torturous. I needed to concentrate on getting home, and then Gavin and I would go back to being strangers again. All that mattered was seeing Ava and my family.

All that matters is making it home so she won't get sick again.

I cursed myself for the nagging worry over that fucked-up dream. But no matter how often I reminded myself it wasn't real, it was like I could feel the hospital tiles under my feet and the helpless grief that had doubled me over as the doctor shook his head.

Shivering, I turned the heat up a notch, glancing at Gavin as he shifted and licked his lips before settling again.

Fuck, I didn't want to think about him either, but the road was flat and straight, and my traitorous mind wandered back to that Labor Day weekend before the first day of ninth grade.

It hadn't rained in two weeks, and the cloying humidity couldn't save the lawns of Tremont Street from their yellowed fate. Watering was only allowed every other evening, and we couldn't even turn on the sprinkler for a few minutes to run through it.

Of course Gavin and I had gone to the pond on the other side of the preserve as usual, and were almost there when the storm clouds had lumbered over. We had the place to ourselves after a while as the other kids scrambled home, lightning streaking the sky.

We'd stretched out on our backs in a low grassy nook at the edge of the pond, safely away from the trees. I swear we could feel the thunder rumble through the earth, and the rain flooded down, soaking us. It had been Sunday, and even though school started Tuesday, it had felt years away that afternoon as we opened our mouths to catch raindrops.

The odd snowflake drifted down onto the blacktop as I drove on. I turned down the radio to a low murmur, listening to Gavin's breathing. Red Bull was tart on my tongue as memories wove through my mind.

It'd rained that afternoon for an hour—bucketing down, as my grandma would have said. Our shorts and T-shirts clung to us when the sun blazed out of the clouds. Gavin's hair had dried while we laid there, and that was the day I finally hadn't been able to resist reaching out to run my fingers through it.

The humid tension in the air that the rain had banished returned in a blink. Gavin watched me with wide eyes, not moving back from my touch. My brain screamed at me to stop, but as his lips parted, I lurched over and kissed him. Our noses bumped and he squeaked, but he miraculously didn't push me away. We mashed our lips together, and my dick got so hard I thought I'd come right then.

We rolled onto our sides in the long grass at the water's edge, kissing hard, our tongues thrusting awkwardly now. Pressing closer, hands reaching for skin—

"Cowabunga!"

Even now, my heart skipped a beat at the memory of the splash as one of the Warner boys from two blocks over took a running leap off a rock and into the pond. We'd bolted to our feet and barely looked at each other, rushing into the water to hide our boners.

"Oh, hey!" Joey Warner said. "Thought I was the only one here."

"Nope!" I laughed too loudly: ha-ha-ha. I snuck a glance at Gav beside me, but he was treading water and looking down at the ripples spreading across the surface.

"Charlie, you hear Pete Stiffler's parents are still out of town? He's having a party tonight. There might even be beer!"

Gavin frowned. "We probably shouldn't drink. We might get in trouble."

"Don't worry, Saint Gavin." I gave him a smile. "We'll be okay."

I pulled around a truck and moved back into the right lane. When I glanced at Gavin now, the resentment bubbled up. I knew it was me who kissed him, and I guess he'd just been too nice or too horny to push me away. I shouldn't blame him for that.

But that night as we'd walked to Pete Stiffler's house, he'd kissed me quickly in the shadows with a shy smile and whispered, "Let's go back to the pond tomorrow."

We never did.

As I followed the straight yellow lines of the highway with Gavin sleeping inches away, it somehow hurt more than ever.

Three

Gavin

December 22ⁿᵈ

"Son of a fucking bitch!"

I jerked up. My mouth was dry and I licked my lips, blinking at Charlie. "What's wrong?"

"Can't you feel that? Something happened to the tire."

He was slowing, and I realized, yes, there was a dragging tug on the right side of the car. As Charlie pulled onto the shoulder, I peered around. There was nothing but darkness in any direction, aside from two lonely headlights in the distance on the other side of the road. And the world was white, but it wasn't salt this time. I stared at the snow. "Where are we?"

"Wyoming. Shit!" Charlie slammed the heel of his hand against the steering wheel. "Guess you don't have gloves or anything either?"

"No. All my winter gear's at home. I figured I'd buy some on the way." According to the clock, it was three-forty-seven, but I wasn't sure if that was still on California time. We'd apparently passed Salt Lake City and all the mountains, and were back on flat land. At least the highway and shoulder had been plowed, and the foot of snow covering the expanse of land stretching out in every direction didn't seem fresh.

Charlie's shoulders hitched as he took a deep breath and pulled up his hood, zipping his hoodie right to the top. "Okay. I'm going to look." He turned his head to check the road—still empty—and opened the door, leaving the engine running.

The blast of winter air had me shivering in point-two seconds, and I tugged my leather jacket back on before joining him. The bitter wind rasped my ears, and I shoved my hands in my pockets as I leaned over the front tire where Charlie crouched.

"Goddamn it!" He stood and kicked the flattening tire.

My heart sank. There was no way we could drive much farther on that thing, and I didn't remember seeing a spare in the trunk. I hurried around to double check. "No spare." I used my phone flashlight to examine the trunk. "Not even a jack. Isn't that stuff supposed to be in here?"

"I dunno. Never rented a car before. Fuck!"

"It's okay. We'll call…" I held my phone up, spinning in a circle. The dreaded words remained on the top of the screen.

No service

"We'll have to flag someone down." I peered along the empty highway, my teeth chattering.

"What if we can't get it fixed?" Charlie stood by the damaged tire, staring at it. "I have to make it back."

"We still have a few days. It'll be fine."

He didn't seem to really hear me. Shaking his head, he crossed his arms over his chest, hugging himself. I barely heard his whisper. "Fuck. If I don't get there…"

Charlie screwed his eyes shut, and he looked so much younger in that moment as he trembled. I leaned closer, and in the glow of the headlights, I realized a tear had escaped the squeeze of his eyelids. My breath caught in my throat. I froze.

Charlie was crying?

I'd never seen him cry before, and I *hated* it. It hurt in a way I hadn't thought possible. I was afraid to say anything, but I had to. "What is it?"

"Nothing," he croaked, shaking his head again, his eyes still shut. Before I could really think about it, I reached out. I felt the hardness of his shoulder bone through the cotton of his hoodie, and he sucked in a breath. "Don't. Please."

"It's okay. Everything's going to be okay." He shivered violently, and I tentatively rubbed his back, my fingers going numb in the icy bite of the wind. "We'll get it fixed. You must have driven over something back there, and—"

Charlie spun out of my reach, swiping at his eyes with choppy movements. "So it's my fault? I didn't see anything! How am I supposed to see out here?"

I blinked and stepped back. It was like a switch had been flicked and Charlie had slammed a door on his feelings. I hated to see it just as much as the tears. "Of course it's not your fault. I didn't say that."

"But you meant it." He tugged his phone from his pocket and tapped it on.

I clenched my jaw. "*No*, that's not what I meant at all. I was just saying that something must have punctured the tire. It would have happened the same if I'd been driving. Don't put words in my mouth. Relax. We'll figure it out."

His harsh laugh cut through me like the whipping wind. "Relax? We're in the middle of nowhere with no cell service."

"We'll flag someone down eventually."

"And what? Think they'll give us a spare tire?" He jabbed his phone again, shaking his head. "I should have known this would be a disaster. Because of course it is. It involves you."

I crossed my arms tightly. "Oh, so it's *my* fault now?" Apparently the cold had frozen my brain and I'd forgotten what a jerk he could be. Why should I feel sorry for him? Hardening myself, I concentrated on the old resentment bubbling up. "What are you going to do? Punch me again?"

Charlie's head snapped up, his eyes glittering furiously. "Maybe I will. I'm sure *Candace* will kiss it all better."

Our breath huffed out in angry clouds in the frigid air. "Don't talk about her. I don't know what she ever did to you—"

"Are you serious right now?" Incredulous, he stared at me. "You know exactly what she did. What *you* did."

I shook my head. "None of it was her fault. I know… I know it was crappy how things went down back in ninth grade, but it's no excuse for treating her like that. And I fucked up, but that doesn't give you the right to break my nose! You're just lucky I told my parents I got hit with a lacrosse stick. I could have had you arrested for that sucker punch."

He pressed his lips together in a thin line. "You shouldn't have done me any favors, Saint Gavin."

"Don't call me that!" Exhaust fumes from the car blew around my knees, and I wanted to scream. "I know I've made mistakes, but that day in the pizza place I never even said a word to you."

"You laughed!" His words rang out sharply.

"So? You dropped your slice and spilled your soda all over the floor. Everyone laughed! It was no big deal!"

"*Everyone* wasn't the first guy I ever kissed! *Everyone* didn't break my fucking heart."

Standing there by the side of the deserted road with dawn and home feeling like a lifetime away, we stared at each other, our chests heaving and fists clenched. Regret collided with a burst of sticky shame, and I wished so much that I could go back and be brave.

Charlie hunched his shoulders, his head dropping. I could barely hear him now. "There you were with your perfect girlfriend and all your popular friends, and you hadn't even *looked* at me in years. But you were looking at me then. *Laughing* at me."

My anger was lost in the wind, carried away across the vast emptiness surrounding us. I shivered. "I didn't mean…" I shook my head. "Charlie…"

He was already circling the car and climbing in. I got in the passenger side, glad of the warmth if nothing else. We both held our hands to the air vents as I tried to find the right words.

"You're right. It was a dick thing to do. It was. I'm sorry. If I could take it back, I would. But please don't blame Candace. I know you hate me, but she never did anything wrong. She never…she doesn't know about us, Charlie. I never told her."

The rush of the hot air blasting from the vents was the only sound aside from our shallow breathing. After a few heartbeats, Charlie spoke quietly, his gaze on the steering wheel. "I shouldn't have hit you or said those epically shitty things to her. I know that. I'm sorry I did it. I owe her an apology. I wanted to tell her a bunch of times, but I let myself be bitter instead. It was easier to just hate the world than deal."

"Yeah." The words grated out of my throat. "I know something about being afraid to deal."

His voice was barely a whisper. "You shouldn't have dumped me like that. You didn't know anyone when you moved to Norwalk, and I was your friend. But then you got in with Candace and the popular kids, and overnight I was nothing to you. I know you're not…even if you didn't like me the same way, you were still my friend." He took a shaky breath. "You were the best friend I ever had. No one got me the way you did."

My throat was too tight to say anything, and blood rushed in my ears. I reached out, my fingers grazing his by the vent, the hot air giving me pins and needles. "Charlie, I…"

A honk made us both jump, and I jerked my hand back. Red taillights appeared as a pickup truck passed by and then backed up on the shoulder. All the things I needed to say were breaking loose, but Charlie was already out of the car again, jogging over to the truck before I could form a sentence. I followed.

"You boys need a hand?" An older man climbed out of the cab.

"We've got a flat. Don't suppose you have a spare?" Charlie asked. "We'd call triple-A, but there's no signal."

The man whistled. "Oh, you'd be waiting an awful long time for them to show up, even if you could call." He squinted at the Jetta. "I've got a spare, but it'd be too big. I have a hitch on the back, so I can tow you a ways down the track to Little America. There's a garage there that should be able to fix you up come morning."

"Little America?" I asked.

"Yep. It's named after the hotel. Old Earl Holding built the first one out here in the middle of nowhere decades ago. Now there are about seventy of us who live around the hotel. It's a bit of an oasis for travelers like yourselves. We were the world's biggest gas station for a while—fifty-five pumps. But now there's a Buc-ee's down in Texas with sixty." He chuckled. "There's talk we might go to sixty-one, just for the hell of it. All right, let's get you hitched up. Oh, and I'm Bill."

After introducing ourselves, Charlie and I hovered around fairly uselessly as Bill went about hitching the Jetta to his truck. Finally he shooed us into the cab, scolding us for our lack of winter gear. Charlie slid into the middle and I followed him, settling into the right side of the truck. My ears stung from the cold, and I blew on my hands.

There was so much I wanted to say, but now the words had slithered down into nooks and crannies like water over rocks. I cleared my throat and managed to say, "I think we—"

"Forget it. It's fine. We need to concentrate on getting home. It was all a long time ago. It doesn't matter now anyway, right?"

I looked at his Adam's apple bob as he rubbed his hands, and my fingers itched to touch. I wasn't even sure where, exactly. *Everywhere.* I'd watched him grow up from a distance, and being next to Charlie now make me tingle all over. It mattered so much that it stole my breath.

Then Bill was climbing into the driver's seat, and we were on our way to a place called Little America.

Charlie

"You're in luck—I've got a double left." The desk clerk—Stephen—tapped his computer. "I'll just need a credit card."

I worked on a reasonable tone. "A double? We actually need a room with two beds."

Stephen did the dreaded closed-mouth smile/head tilt combo, and I sagged against the counter. "So sorry, gentlemen. It's our annual Little America Christmas Festival this weekend. This is literally the last room in the hotel."

Gavin asked, "There are no other hotels in town?"

Stephen smiled. "We *are* the town."

I passed over my credit card, since clearly we were out of options and we might as well try for a couple hours of sleep. Bill had towed us to the garage by the seriously enormous gas station, and we'd walked over to the hotel, which was really a sprawling motel. The whole complex was truly in the middle of nowhere. "And you said you'll leave a message for the garage about fixing our tire?"

"Sure will." Stephen handed over a long envelope with two key cards tucked inside. "Now when you go out the door, turn right. You'll see our travel center right behind the Santa's village. The center's open twenty-four hours, and you'll be able to get hot food there if you'd like. And your room is just down this way." He pointed to a laminated map of the complex that sat on the counter.

"Do they sell hats and gloves there?" Gavin asked. "This was an unexpected trip."

"You might have better luck in the gift shop, which opens at six-thirty." Stephen glanced at a clock on the wall. "Not too long now."

"Great. Thanks." Gavin smiled wanly.

"And there will be plenty of fun activities in the morning! Candy cane hunt, ice skating on our pond, and our world-famous Reindeer Race."

"Sounds great," I lied. "Thank you."

Outside, we trudged along, dragging our suitcases. This *sucked*. We'd finally been making up some time and getting somewhere. And then I'd had to go dredging up all that stuff. I knew it was wrong that I'd punched Gavin that day. And now I couldn't get Candace's wide-eyed gasp out of my mind, or Gavin's blood spilling over her yellow blouse as she cradled his head.

"Charlie, what's the matter with you? Why did you do that?"

I couldn't answer. Everyone stared at me like I was a freak. "Fuck you, you stupid bitch." I spat out the worst word I could think of. "Cunt."

I'd hated myself the moment I said it, and my next thought was how ashamed my parents would be. And I'd hurt Gavin, who stared at me in shock, holding his hand to his nose as blood poured out. It didn't matter what he'd done to me. I was such an asshole that day, and now my cheeks burned with more than the cold as we neared the fluorescent travel center.

When I'd run out of the pizzeria that day, everyone had only stared, the hisses of their whispers slithering after me. I'd already stopped hanging out with people at school; with Ava so sick, I didn't want to talk to anyone about anything.

After word spread about what I'd done to Gavin, people started actively avoiding me, and I just kept my head down and my earbuds in. I couldn't blame them. And how could I blame Gavin for leaving me in the dust in ninth grade? He'd clearly been better off.

Tim had been… Well, if I was being honest with myself, Tim had been a distraction. We fooled around and chilled, and never really talked about anything. He was a nice guy whose main passions in life were smoking up and killing video game zombies. He liked having sex with me, and it was nice to feel wanted. We had some good times, but I found I didn't miss him. Out of sight, out of mind.

At college, getting off with a guy was fine, but anything more than that made me want to hole up in my dorm. Thank Christ I'd gotten a single. And now here I was, stuck sharing a room with the only guy I'd let get to me.

I rubbed my face as we crossed Little America. Fuck, I just needed to get home for Christmas and keep my promise to Ava. *Can't let her get sick again*, a little voice whispered, and I shoved it away, because that stupid dream wasn't real.

As if to argue, my mind kindly flashed images of the empty hospital bed, stripped of its sheets, the sorrowful doctor, and my Ava gone, gone, gone. Shuddering, I wished I could bleach my brain and scrub away the memories of that goddamned dream.

"I think I'm just going to go to bed." Gavin stopped at the turn for our room.

"Yeah. I'm not hungry either."

So off we went with our heads down as the wind howled, our suitcase wheels rumbling on the pavement. Gavin opened the door and flipped on the lights. "Whoa. This is…"

"Retro?" I stared at the gold-patterned arm chair, which was only missing a plastic cover for the truly authentic grandmother feel. The bedspread matched and the rug was shag green.

"I guess they're going for that nostalgia thing." His gaze fell on the bed. "I can sleep on the floor if you want. It'll only be a few hours anyway."

Part of me really wanted to take him up on that. "No, that's…it's fine. We're adults now, right? And like you said, it's only a few hours."

"Yeah. Of course."

God or whoever the hell is listening, please let the garage have us back on the road soon. I toed off my shoes as Gavin took his turn in the bathroom. I read the hotel information card and tried not to look at the bed.

At least we'd seemed to have formed a truce. I cringed as I thought of how weak I'd been on the side of the road. Ugh, he'd seen me *cry*, and the humiliation was acidy on my tongue. It was easier when I let myself hate him. Easier when we never spoke, and I could forget the concerned timber of his voice and the weight of his sympathetic hand. And how much I'd wanted to be in his arms and let the tears fall.

What the hell was wrong with me? Ava was fine. I had to get my shit together. I'd never really been superstitious, and I needed to let go of this dream.

In a faded green tee and boxers, Gavin came out and climbed under the sheets on the side closest to the door. I flipped off the lights and took my sweet time in the shower, hoping he'd be passed out when I finally I tiptoed into the dark room. The curtains were open a few inches, giving me enough light to find my way.

I gingerly sat on the side of the bed and shimmied under the covers as quietly as I could. Gavin was curled away from me on his side, and I mirrored his pose, keeping my back to him. Willing myself to relax, I waited for the world to fade away.

The silence was too heavy, and I knew Gavin wasn't asleep. I resolutely closed my eyes. Seriously, what was the point in rehashing everything? We were stuck together on this trip, and then we'd go back to never speaking again. We'd only been friends for a couple months after he moved to Norwalk. We were strangers now.

So why did I want to roll over and press against him, breathe him in and taste him? I'd been with other guys. Why was this one so deep under my skin? They say you never forget your first, but this was ridiculous. It wasn't as though we'd had some big romance. One day of fumbling and kissing should have been long forgotten.

Even if it had destroyed me back then, we were kids. It shouldn't mean anything now.

Gavin shifted slightly and I held my breath. I could feel the heat of his body only a few inches away, and I was already in serious danger of falling off my side of the bed. I listened to Gavin not-sleep and watched the minutes slowly tick by on the LCD alarm clock. It was already technically morning, but dawn could not come fast enough.

Gavin

Drifting in a limbo world between sleeping and waking, my whole body was tense and my legs were nearly pulled up to my chest. My hair was damp with night sweats, and even though I knew I needed real sleep, it wasn't going to happen. I supposed a couple hours of half sleep would have to do, and I opened my eyes to the faded gray morning edging through the gap in the curtains.

Behind me, Charlie snored faintly. I inched over onto my back and extended my cramped legs, pointing and flexing my toes as I watched him. He'd turned over at some point, and his hand nearly brushed my arm. His lips were parted, and God, I knew it was a cliché, but he looked so innocent.

Without the angry set of his jaw and the tight hunch of his shoulders, he reminded me so much of the Charlie I'd known that first summer. The Charlie who'd been my friend until I'd ruined it.

Until I broke his heart.

He murmured and smacked his lips before falling still again, and I wondered what it would be like to kiss him now. That day at the pond, it had been a frenzy of shoving ourselves together as our hormones exploded like cherry bombs at our heels. I wanted to kiss him slowly now—tease open his lips and feel the slide of his tongue as the rasp of his faint stubble rubbed against mine.

I sucked in a breath. Shit, I should *not* be thinking about these things with morning wood that was all too eager. My pulse raced and I couldn't look away from him. It was warm in the room, and he'd kicked the comforter down to his feet.

His white tee had ridden up to reveal a few inches of belly and the dark hair that disappeared in a trail below his waistband. Hair dusted his legs as well, and his left knee was bent a bit, displaying a mole on his inner thigh that I wanted to lick. I could see the bulge of his cock through his plaid boxers, and I wondered what it would be like to take him in my mouth and suck.

Lust and terror tightened my balls. Shit, I should have had the guts to hook up with guys at school; maybe I wouldn't be wound so freaking tight. But I'd been too chicken. I thought of Candace just before she left for New York, nudging me with her elbow.

"When are you going to go for it? Just jump in with both feet. And hands. And…" She leaned in close and whispered, *"And your, you know—dick. It'll be awesome!"*

But she was wrong. Sex with her the few times we'd done it had been awkward and never really *right*, but it hadn't scared me. Maybe because I'd known her so well. Or because I'd been going through the motions for so long that it was just one more performance. And I genuinely cared about Candace, and had wanted her first time to be good for her. I'd been so focused on that, I'd ignored what I'd really wanted.

The truth was, the thought of actually fucking another guy in real life and not just in my fevered fantasies was absolutely, positively petrifying. Never mind the fact that it was *Charlie* I was perving on right now. Because even as I tried to convince myself that it was just dick I craved, I knew it was a lie.

It was Charlie I wanted to touch and taste. I wanted it then, and I wanted it now. But after what'd happened, Charlie could never like me again, and I couldn't blame him.

My silent phone on the side table lit up, and I reached for it and read my dad's text, glad for the distraction.

How's the journey going? You're okay for money?

I tapped the keyboard with my thumbs and answered:

Everything's good, and yes. Just waking up in Wyoming. Say hi to Mom. Hope it's warmer there than it is here! :)

Dad's answer was a picture of a gorgeous white sand beach and blue ocean with a glorious sun rising above it. He added:

Drive carefully and give our love to Candace. We'll see you when you get back from the slopes. Stay safe, kiddo.

I turned off my phone and sighed. I hadn't mentioned the tire problem or that Charlie was with me, because then Dad would have all sorts of questions I didn't want to answer. Questions he didn't want to ask.

Since I'd gone to college, my parents and I had talked about my classes, and the weather, and Mom's book club, and Dad's bowling league, and none of the things that really mattered. Mom clearly wanted me to get back with Candace, but she didn't even ask if I'd met any other girls. Dad certainly didn't either.

I admit it—when Candace and I called it quits, I'd waited for my dad to talk to me about why. Talk to me about being gay. It was still weird to think it: *I'm gay. I'm really, truly, gay.*

I thought for sure he'd sit me down one day and we'd hash it all out. I waited. And waited. Then it was suddenly the day I was leaving for Stanford, and we'd only talked about my job at the local pool, the Red Sox's pennant chances, and a bunch of stuff that didn't mean anything.

I squeezed my eyes shut as I thought of that Labor Day Monday in the garage four years ago, the morning after I kissed a boy and then a girl. The morning I didn't know what the hell to do, because it was the boy I really, really wanted to kiss again. Dad had always been my best friend. He'd always told me the right things. He always knew best.

"Don't tell your mother."

Charlie shifted again, moaning as he woke, and the weight of everything I'd missed out on the last four years bore down like I was plummeting to the bottom of the ocean. I sprang out of bed and into the bathroom, turning on the shower full blast so he wouldn't hear me cry.

Four

Gavin

"Okay. Thank you." Charlie hung up the phone on the table beside the bed as I came out of the bathroom, dressed and shaved. "It'll be ready by eleven. Apparently they're busy with a couple of trucks first. Should you call the rental company? They'd better be paying us back for this tire."

"We got the insurance, so I hope so. I'll call them later. Sorry if I took a long time in the bathroom."

"It's cool. Apparently we're not in a rush."

"I saw a sign about a pancake breakfast as part of this festival thing. You want to check it out?"

"Sure." Charlie unzipped his enormous pink suitcase and rooted around, pulling out a bunch of Transformers, weirdly enough. "I'm going to grab another shower." He tugged out a pair of boxers from the bottom of his suitcase. "You don't have to wait."

"I don't mind. I'm not starving." I sat on the bed against the headboard and flipped on the TV. Like he said, we were adults now. We could be civil and normal. "Maybe we could build Optimus Prime after breakfast."

He smiled tentatively. "Those are for Ava."

I smiled back. "Cool. I'm sure she'll love them." I picked at a stray thread on the rumpled comforter. "Is she…you said she's in remission?"

Charlie had picked up one of the Transformer boxes, and now he spun it in his hands. "Yeah. I gave her my bone marrow, and it worked. She had to do a lot of chemo and crap, but it worked."

"You donated your bone marrow?"

His brows drew together, his voice small. "You really think I wouldn't?"

"No, no, of course you would. I just didn't know is all."

He exhaled and ran a hand through his messy hair. "Right. Well, yeah, I donated my marrow, and she's better." He fiddled with the box again, his gaze locked on it. "For now, at least."

There were a million things I wanted to say, but the words wouldn't come. Instead I asked, "You didn't take time off school, did you? For the bone marrow?"

"Only a day. It didn't take long. I was just tired and stuff. I slept a lot for a weekend, and then I was fine."

"Did it hurt?"

"Like a son of a bitch. I had a local, but afterward it ached a lot. Only for a couple days, though." He turned at the foot of the bed and lifted his tee. "I have a little tiny scar from one of the incisions." He tugged his boxers lower on his hips. "See?"

My heart drummed as I crawled down the mattress and peered at his lower back. On the left side, I could see the faint line, and I reached out with a fingertip before I could stop myself. As I traced it, I thought I felt him shiver. "Sorry—cold hands."

"It's okay," he muttered in a strangled voice.

"You said it only hurt for a little while? This doesn't hurt, does it?" I stopped the motion of my finger, but didn't pull my hand back.

Charlie shook his head, facing away from me.

"They took it from your hip bone?" I asked.

"Yeah." He stood frozen as I inspected the scar, running my finger over the pale skin.

"You said she's better for now. Is there a chance it'll come back?"

"Always a chance. Especially if I—" He dropped his shirt and spun away, rifling through the clothes in his suitcase and not looking at me.

"If you what?" Sitting on my feet at the end of the bed, I watched his jerky movements. I wanted to touch more of him so badly I clenched my hands.

After a deep breath, he said, "I just have to get back soon."

"Or what? What's going to happen if you miss Christmas? I mean, I know it'll suck big time for all of you, but it seems like there's more to it. What are you afraid of?"

Still not looking at me, Charlie straightened and addressed the jeans in his hands. "It's dumb. I know it is. But I can't get it out of my head."

"What is it?"

His cheeks puffed as he blew out a noisy breath. "I dreamed that I didn't make it home in time for Christmas and Ava died."

I winced. "That's awful. I'm sorry. But a dream doesn't have to mean anything. I don't think they ever do."

Staring at the jeans clutched in his hands, he nodded. "It felt so real, though. I can remember it like it happened. Smell the antiseptic from the hospital."

I wanted to move closer to him, but I was afraid he'd stop talking. "I hate nightmares like that."

"Yeah. The only reason I left for school was because she was in remission. I never would have gone otherwise. I still hated leaving her, but they gave me a scholarship, and Mom and Dad insisted I should live my life. But I can't imagine life without her. And when I told her I was leaving…" He inhaled deeply.

"That must have been rough."

Charlie folded and unfolded the jeans, still not looking at me. "Yeah. She tried to be brave the way she is so much of the time, but I'd always, always been there, you know? And I promised I'd be back for Christmas since we couldn't afford Thanksgiving flights too, and Christmas is a longer break. I know it seems like we should have a ton of money since my dad's a lawyer, but even with insurance, the medical bills have been brutal."

"God, I can only imagine."

"I promised. I looked her in the eye and I swore I'd be back for Christmas. The last two years, she was so bad she was in the hospital all the time. This is her first Christmas back at home, and we were going to open our stockings together in the middle of the night, and then wake up our parents and—" He rubbed his face. "Just do all that stuff that we did before she got sick."

"You will. We'll get there. We still have time. I'll get you there." If I had to piggyback him the way he did Ava, I'd make it happen.

Nodding, he exhaled shakily. "Thanks. I don't know why I'm such a basket case. Sorry."

"Don't be sorry." I got up and chanced a step toward him. "It's totally understandable."

"If something happened to her and I wasn't there, I don't know what I'd do," he whispered.

"It's okay." I reached for his shoulder, squeezing gently. "It's okay to be scared. You're allowed. You don't have to be fearless all the time."

He trembled, shaking his head. "*Me?* I'm afraid of everything."

"Could've fooled me."

Our eyes locked. "Guess I did."

My hand still rested on his shoulder, and I leaned closer, the vulnerability in his blue eyes drawing me like a magnet. "Charlie…"

He bent over suddenly, grabbing even more clothes from his suitcase. "I just need to shake it off." He gave his arms and legs a wriggle as he stood, and then looked at me, his cheeks going red. "Uh, it's this thing Ava and I do. When she was going through chemo, it was like our little…I dunno. Ritual, I guess. A lot of times she was too weak to even stand, so I'd shake it off for her. All the bad stuff she was feeling. It's dumb."

My chest tightened. "It's not dumb at all." I hated that he'd gone through so much with Ava and that I hadn't even *tried* to be there for him. I kicked my feet and shook my arms. "Here, I'll help."

He smiled then, a beam that lit up his face as he chuckled. "Thanks, Gav."

Oh God, my heart swelled like the Grinch's, almost busting through my chest. To hear him call me *Gav* again after so long, I just… It meant a lot. I managed to keep my voice steady. "No prob."

"Thanks. Um if you're hungry now, go ahead."

Obviously I wasn't going anywhere. I sat on the bed again and flipped through the TV channels, and when Charlie came out after his shower, we both pretended like everything was fine. Which it was. It was just…weird, but not in a bad way.

We hit the gift shop first, and soon we were outfitted in ridiculously matching Little America fleeces, mitts, and woolen caps with a pom-pom on the top. They were all navy blue with red and white accents. We looked spectacularly lame, but we'd be warm.

After Charlie bought Ava a snow globe, we walked across the complex to the outdoor breakfast. Jaunty Christmas music blared from a loudspeaker near Santa's village, and we lined up for our pancakes. People milled around in Santa suits and more Christmas sweaters than I knew existed in the world.

The wind had died, so it was nice, even if it was overcast. Snowflakes drifted down, and I found myself humming to "Jingle Bell Rock." I'd always enjoyed the bright lights and fun songs of Christmas. Adam Sandler had done his best to fill the void, but Christmas totally had Hanukkah beat on music.

We sat at a picnic table covered with a red and green tablecloth and dug into our pancakes and maple syrup with plastic utensils. I moaned. "Mmm. This is good. I haven't had pancakes in forever."

"Me either." Charlie took another bite. "I haven't had real maple syrup in ages. Ava likes the fake stuff better. Strange, I know."

I pointed to his chin. "You've got…" Charlie's tongue swept out and caught the stray drop of syrup, and my belly somersaulted.

"What?" He frowned. "Didn't I get it?" He wiped his mouth with a napkin. "Is it gone now?"

"Uh-huh." I shoved another forkful into my mouth and concentrated on my plate instead of the dexterity of Charlie's tongue. "Do you still read *The Walking Dead*?"

"Of course. You?"

I nodded. "The last issue was crazy. I wonder if they'll go that far on the show?"

"Probably. They already did cannibals, so I don't think they're afraid to go there. I just hope they don't kill off Daryl."

"Nah. He's too popular. But I guess I wouldn't put it past them either."

"I've got a theory about how the rest of the season will go." Charlie's eyes lit up as he spoke, and he cut into his pancakes with gusto.

As he spun out his theory for me, I was hit again with a wave of longing for the years we'd missed out on, and all the conversations we could have had about zombies and comics and cannibals. That summer when we met, we rode our bikes around the neighborhood in a big loop, pedaling side by side on the quiet streets and talking about…everything.

"Anyway. It probably won't happen, but wouldn't it be *awesome*?"

I grinned. "Totally."

Charlie looked at me for a long moment, and then ducked his head, the pom-pom on his hat wobbling.

"What?" I asked, frowning. "Do I have something on my face?" I wiped my mouth with my napkin.

He glanced up from his plate. "Yep. You got it."

A woman wearing a sweater and matching woolen hat festooned with elves appeared by our table holding a clipboard. "Merry Christmas, boys! Are you signed up for the Reindeer Run?"

I smiled at her. "Merry Christmas. No, we're actually just here for the morning. Our car had a flat."

"Well, you're in luck! The race starts in twenty minutes. It's all for charity. The more entrants we have, the more money goes to provide gifts for needy kids in Cheyenne. You don't have to pay to take part—we just need your athletic prowess. What do you say?"

Charlie and I looked at each other. He shrugged. "Sure. I guess a little run won't kill us, especially if it's for a good cause. It's not far, is it? We have to get back on the road as soon as we can."

She pointed across the complex to where a red and green banner was being erected. "Just across the lot. You'll have plenty of time. Let me get your names." She jotted down the info on her clipboard and passed us two plastic race bibs, both with the number thirty-six.

"Oh, don't we need different numbers?" I asked.

"Nope! You'll be racing as a team. See you at the start line in fifteen minutes!" She bustled off.

We looked at each other and shrugged. "Sounds easy enough," Charlie said, peering at the expanse of the parking lot where the racetrack was being set up. "That'll be a really quick race."

Before long, we stood at the starting line in our ridiculous hats with our race numbers on over our matching fleeces. I stared at a race organizer, a man in a Santa suit. "Wait, what? Blindfolded? Piggyback?"

Santa laughed with an actual *ho-ho-ho* sound. "See, you're the reindeer and he's the sleigh." Santa nodded to Charlie. "He's got to carry the bags of presents, stay balanced on your back, *and* give you directions. That's the challenge."

"But…I don't remember Rudolph ever being *blindfolded*," I protested.

Santa approached me with a wide strip of gold and red material and tied it around my head.

"Wait. I don't think this is a good idea," I insisted.

"Can you see anything?" Santa asked.

"No! That's why it's a bad idea."

"You're not afraid of the dark, are you? *Ho-ho-ho*. Good luck, boys!" He slapped me lightly on the back and presumably left.

Charlie's voice was thick with amusement. "This is like some twisted Christmas S and M fantasy. Little America is kinky."

"This is ridiculous." I reached up to take off the blindfold, but someone caught my wrist. "Charlie?"

He was closer now, and I thought I could feel the heat of his body brushing close to mine. "It's me. Don't worry, I won't let Santa tie you up in his workshop with the elves. Unless you're into it." His fingers were comforting and solid around my wrist. We'd taken off our mitts to eat breakfast, and without the biting wind, hadn't needed to put them back on.

I wanted to laugh, but my heart thumped violently. He let go of me, and I reached out into open air, exposed and alone. "Charlie?"

His voice was still right there. "Hey, it's okay. Are you freaking out?" He squeezed the back of my neck with his warm hand. "We don't have to do this."

I took a deep breath. "No, it's okay. I just… This is weird, right?"

"Seriously weird. I bet this Christmas extravaganza is actually a secret sex party for people with a Yuletide fetish." He took my arm. "Going to the starting line now." After about ten steps, he stopped. "And here's where things get even weirder. Crouch down so I can jump on. Those kids better appreciate this."

I bent my knees and tipped over, and Charlie's weight landed on my back. I staggered as I stood straight, hefting him up with my arms under his knees. Having him pressed against me sent tingles zipping all over.

"I seriously have to carry this bag?" Charlie asked someone. He dug his fingers into my right shoulder as his left hand lifted.

A woman's voice yelled out, "On your marks, get set—go!" A blare from a bullhorn made me jump, and I started running.

"No, no, go left!" Charlie shouted, and I dutifully veered over. "Not that far!" He bounced around on my back, and I was pretty sure we were going to end up eating concrete. He said something else I couldn't make out over the commands of all the other teams and the cheers I assumed were from onlookers.

"I can't hear you!" I shouted, running as fast as I could even though it didn't matter who won this bizarre race.

Charlie's arm went around my neck, and he tugged up my hat, his lips brushing my ear. "More to the right. Oh shit, that guy's going to hit us! Stop!"

My pulse thrumming, I jolted to a dead halt.

"Okay, run!" His laughter echoed in my ear, his breath hot. "Keep going! A bit to the right."

I found myself laughing too as we zigzagged across the Little America parking lot. I only knew we'd reached the finish line when the warmth of Charlie's weight disappeared.

But as he hopped down, our feet got caught and I tumbled to the ground—which was surprisingly bouncy. Charlie flopped on top of me, and I pulled off the blindfold to see that we'd landed on a long inflatable candy cane they were using as a crash mat.

His weight pressed me down, and I could feel him shaking with laughter. I joined in, and I could have stayed there all day giggling with Charlie on that candy cane. We were all tangled up, and as I squirmed onto my back, he grinned down at me in his silly pom-pom hat, the blue making his eyes pop.

My breath caught. He was so beautiful.

"You okay?" My hat had fallen off, and Charlie ran his hand over my head, his fingers gentle as he smoothed out my undoubtedly messy hair. "I didn't hurt you, did I?"

The weight of his thigh against mine where we sprawled was wonderful and torturous. I shook my head.

There were other runners stumbling over the finish line, and we had to scoot out of the way as a team careened into the candy cane, shrieking with laughter. Charlie pulled me to my feet and held up his hand for a high five. I smacked his palm.

"We totally got beat by the elf lady." He leaned in and lowered his voice. "She clearly knows her way around a blindfold, I'm just saying. Now let's get the hell out of here before they ask us to play any more of their reindeer games."

Charlie

The neon of the twenty-four-hour gas station beckoned us off the interstate just before midnight. I consulted the map on my phone. "We're close to Lincoln. Not bad."

Gavin pulled up to one of the pumps. "Too bad it took until past noon for that new tire. I still need to call the rental company. Ugh. I hate dealing with—" He waved his hand and chuckled. "Grownup stuff. I guess I should get used to it, huh?"

I smiled. "Yeah. Good thing we both have credit cards. My limit's a thousand bucks, so we'd better not blow any more tires."

While Gavin pulled on his fleece and filled up the tank, I shrugged mine over my hoodie, shivering as I headed into the station to stock up our supply of Doritos, sour cream and onion chips, gummy bears, Reese's, Red Bull, and Cokes. I'd slept for a couple hours through the endless, snow-packed flatness of Nebraska, and it was my turn to drive.

Yawning widely, I bought the snacks and headed outside with the bathroom key, regretting not bringing my Little America mitts and hat. I realized I was smiling to myself as I turned around the dark corner of the gas station. After that nutso blindfolded run, things with Gavin had been…pretty cool. Better than. We were maybe friends again and—

My feet flew out from under me, and I cartwheeled my arms uselessly on my way to slamming onto the concrete, the bathroom key and plastic bag sailing from my grasp. I managed to keep my head up on impact, but my lungs didn't work, frozen as the air rushed out of me. Little pebbles dug into the back of my skull as I laid there, and the ground was freezing through my jeans. And apparently motherfucking icy. Good to know.

It was so cold, but I couldn't seem to make my limbs move, or my lungs expand. Everything hurt, and I managed a little gasp and whimper. *Owwww.*

"Charlie? Did you say something?" Gavin's voice was distant. I must have yelped when I fell. I tried to answer, but speech was beyond me in that moment. He called my name again, and then I heard the *thud-thud-thud* of rapidly approaching footsteps. Gavin's face blotted out my view of the Big Dipper beyond the brick side of the gas station. "Charlie! Are you okay?"

I managed to grit out, "Fucking ice."

His face pinched, Gavin gently ran his palm over my head, brushing the back of my skull with his fingertips and sending a shiver down my spine. His breath puffed out over my cheeks, summery sweet in the frosty air. "Does it hurt?" He grimaced. "I mean, of course it hurts. Can you get up? Should I call an ambulance?"

My lungs were hauling in more air now, and I shook my head gingerly as I pushed myself up. My voice was reedy. "I'm okay. Just knocked the wind out of me."

Gavin wrapped his arm around my back. "Are you sure? You might have a concussion." He held up a fist. "How many fingers?"

"None. Nice try." His arm was strong and solid around me, and I leaned into him where he knelt on the concrete. I took a deep breath, and the faint scent of a woodsy cologne mixed with pure Gavin made my head spin. I wished to hell it was a concussion, but it was so much worse.

I shoved myself to my feet, and he gripped my elbow with a smile that dimpled his goddamn cheeks.

"Good thing you've got a hard head, right?"

I managed a smile back before shuffling to the bathroom, which of course was locked. "Can you see the key anywhere?" It still hurt to talk, but everything was loosening up again. Shit, I'd forgotten what it was like having the wind thumped out of you. It had happened all the time in hockey, but I hadn't played since Ava got sick.

Gavin pulled out his phone and turned on the flashlight. "Got it." He unlocked the door for me, which really wasn't necessary. "Are you sure you're okay? Um…do you need help?" He hovered beside me.

Part of me wanted to keep him at arm's length and bite out something sarcastic about having handled my dick without him all these years. But I just quietly said, "I'm good. Thanks."

"Okay. I can keep driving, and we'll see how your head feels."

"I landed on my back. Seriously, I'm fine. I'll pop some ibuprofen."

He twisted his lips. "Let's just make sure. I'll get a Red Bull. It's all good."

"Oh, I bought some. Shit." I eyed the contents of the plastic bag, which were now strewn over the pavement.

"I'll get it all." He carefully picked his way over the icy patch while I leaned in the doorway watching, even though I should hurry up and piss already since we were losing time. Then Gavin turned back, his brow furrowed. "Sure you didn't break anything?"

Not trusting myself to speak, I nodded, and he stooped over to pick up the snacks. It was true—my bones were intact, still knitted tightly together. But in that moment under the brittle expanse of Nebraska winter sky, I knew my heart was doomed all over again.

Gavin

December 23ʳᵈ

It was just before six p.m. when I pulled off the interstate and into a McDonald's parking lot. A headache was coming on, and I'd turned off my nineties hip-hop playlist some miles back. Charlie dozed in the passenger seat, curled toward the window. His T-shirt and fleece rode up a little, and I could see a swath of pale skin, close to the bone marrow scar.

I forced my complete attention back to the road. The sun was gone already, and I rubbed my eyes. We'd driven all night and through a steel-gray day across Iowa, Illinois, and Indiana, switching off sleeping and driving.

I found a spot, but left the engine running for the moment, reluctant to wake Charlie. I had the insane urge to reach over and trace the shell of his ear with my finger. He'd seemed fine after his fall in Lincoln, but a bit more rest wouldn't hurt. Maybe I could just leave the car running while I ducked in to piss and grab a fries and Coke. But I could hear my mother's voice, stridently warning me about the what-ifs. *"What if an axe-murderer steals the car? It only takes two seconds!"*

My smile faded as the pang of hurt echoed through me. What would my mother say if she knew I was here with another gay guy? Or if she knew I was gay at all? What about my dad? What were they going to say when I brought home my first boyfriend? Would I even be able to, or would we keep talking about the weather and the Red Sox, pretending nothing had changed?

Maybe Charlie will end up my boyfriend after all.

I inhaled sharply at the flare of *want* that hit me, and Charlie jerked up, blinking. "What?" He stared at me, and then peered around. "What is it? Where are we?"

"Outskirts of Sandusky. Everything's fine." I turned off the engine. "I just need a little break."

"Ohio?" He smiled, and it tugged on my heart. "Awesome. Last thing I remember is South Bend. How are you doing? I can take a turn driving if you want. We're getting close now. I can't wait to see Ava and my folks." He stretched his neck to one side, wincing.

"You okay?"

"Just a little stiff. Falling down hurts, dude." He rolled his shoulders. "It's cool. Let's get some food and then I'll drive."

"Let me see. Face the door." I turned as much as I could and reached for him, sliding my hands below the collar of his fleece and rubbing his neck gently.

A breathy shudder rippled through him. "Cold hands," he murmured.

"Oh, sorry." I pulled them back and huffed a few warm breaths over my fingers, rubbing quickly. Kneading his muscles again, I asked, "Better?" He squeaked out a response that I thought was a yes. I leaned closer. "Relax. Drop your head."

He did, and after a minute I could feel his shoulders lower. My mom got tension headaches once in a while, and I'd seen my dad give her rubs a bunch of times. I used my thumbs on the knots of his spine, and Charlie exhaled a low moan that went straight to my dick.

Biting my lip, I told myself to stay in control. Charlie was in pain, and that's what this was about.

But as I rubbed and pushed at the knots in his flesh, I couldn't help but wonder what it would be like to touch all of him. To be naked together and run my fingers everywhere.

I jerked back, dropping my hands. My cock strained against the zipper of my jeans, and I was officially pathetic, getting off on helping someone with their stiff muscles. But when Charlie looked back at me, his lips were parted and his eyes were dark, and—

My phone lit up on the console between us, Candace's squinty smile bright on the screen. We both stared at it, and Charlie clenched his jaw. He was already opening the door. "I'll give you some privacy," he muttered.

"Charlie—" But he was already gone, hurrying into the McDonald's. I wanted to chase after him and lay it all out about Candace, but I hadn't talked to her in days. "Hey," I answered.

I could hear the grin in her voice. "Hay is for horses! How are you doing? I just wanted to check in. There's some crappy weather coming, and we want to make sure you don't keep driving through it. If you don't make it back in time, you can just meet us in Vermont. My parents said they'd pay for your bus ticket."

"It's cool, Candace. We're in Ohio. Not far now." Although this mention of "crappy weather" set my gut churning.

"Who's we?"

Shit. I hadn't mentioned Charlie to her when we'd texted since I wasn't sure how she'd take it after the pizzeria incident, and there was no point in upsetting her. She wasn't my girlfriend anymore, but she was still my friend. "Oh, yeah. I was going to explain it all when I see you. I ended up driving with someone from high school. Small world, huh?"

She laughed. "What? Seriously? That's crazy. Who?"

"Uh…Charlie Yates."

Candace was deathly silent for a few moments. "Oh. Well…that's… Um, he lives right on your street, doesn't he? How is he doing? Is his sister better? I heard she was."

It was typical Candace—always kind to everyone. I had to swallow hard as my throat tightened with a swell of affection. "Yeah, she's in remission. But he promised her he'd be home for Christmas, so I let him come with me."

"That's nice of you. Is he…have you been seeing him out there?" She was trying to sound casual, something she'd always been terrible at.

I had to chuckle. "No. We ran into each other at the rental agency at the airport right after I got the last car. It was one of those weird coincidences. You should know, he feels really bad about what happened. He said he owes you an apology. It was…he should never have said what he did to you. It was not okay. But he's not a bad person."

"It wasn't okay to punch you either, for the record." She was quiet for a moment. "I guess if you say he's not a bad person, I believe you. I know he was going through a super hard time back then."

"You're really amazing, you know that? I miss you so much."

"I miss you too, sweetie. Am I still allowed to call you that?"

"Always."

"Cool. I need to get your advice on my boy problems when you get home. College dating is very complicated."

"And you think *I* can help? You must be desperate."

"Well, maybe it's time you started dating. Because I'm told that part of the whole benefit of having your high school sweetheart turn out gay is that he gives you inside tips and advice about men. So I expect you to brush up, okay?"

I laughed. "Yes, ma'am."

"Is Charlie still seeing that guy?"

"No. They broke up." I knew I should say more, and I tried to find the words. "It's been… I'm glad I'm getting to know him again. We were really good friends that summer before ninth grade."

The silence dragged out. "Oh. I never knew that."

"It was…complicated. And the way it ended—the way *I* ended our friendship—was messed up. Because we were more than just friends. He didn't punch me for nothing that day at the pizza place."

"Wow. I guess I should have figured that out, huh?"

"No. I should have been honest with you. A lot sooner than I was. I'm sorry."

"We all make mistakes." She sighed. "I'm not going to pretend it doesn't hurt to hear this. But it is what it is, right? We can't change the past. Drive safe, okay? Check that weather report. And… Well, say hi to Charlie for me."

"You really are the most awesome girl in the world, you know that?"

"Maybe I'll get that on a T-shirt and wear it around campus."

"Is this were I give you dating advice and tell you not to do that?"

Her peal of laughter warmed me all the way through. "You're getting it already."

We said goodbye, and I hurried inside to find Charlie. I found him standing just inside the door, watching a TV screen on the wall. A swirling red cloud of doom hovered over the Midwest, creeping out to the East Coast. *Shit.* The headline on the bottom of the screen shouted:

SNOWMAGEDDON RETURNS

My heart sank. "Charlie…"

But he was already walking out. I followed as he strode to the other side of the huge parking lot, which was mostly empty. As if to prove the dire forecast right, snowflakes started coming down. We were both wearing our fleeces, but neither of us had remembered our hats and mitts. I tugged my sleeves over my hands. The wind was completely still. I could smell the snow coming—that unmistakable moisture in the air—as the storm clouds gathered to blot out the stars.

Charlie stopped at the edge of the lot. A snowy field stretched out into the distance, and the hum of the highway behind us was the only noise in the night. Charlie wrapped his arms around himself, facing the farmland.

"We won't make it. I'm not going to be there for Christmas morning. She'll have to open her stocking without me. I promised her, but I'm not going to be there." His tone was flat and lifeless.

"They might be wrong. We might—"

"They're not wrong." He was eerily calm. "You saw that weather system on the screen. There's no way we can go fast enough, even if we can keep driving."

He was right—getting back to Norwalk in that storm was pretty much impossible. "I'm sorry. But Ava will be fine. It was just a dream, Charlie. She's okay. You've done everything you could."

"Yeah. I still just..." He cleared his throat. "It's fine. You're right. I guess you'll be late getting to Vermont. Is Candace upset?"

"Vermont doesn't matter." I closed the distance between us and stood behind him. After a deep breath, I brought my hands to his shoulders. "I'm so sorry about Christmas."

He bowed his head, and I wanted to press my lips to the back of his neck. "Please don't."

I frowned. "What did I do?"

Spinning out of my grasp, Charlie stumbled back a few steps to the edge of a hard snowbank the plow had created. "*This!*" He gestured at me. "Don't be nice! It makes it so much harder."

"You'd rather I be an asshole?" Apparently I couldn't win.

"Yes!" His breath puffed out in a white cloud, his voice rising. "Because otherwise I want to kiss you so fucking much it's like a, a stomach flu—like I'm going to vomit, and I'm sweating and shaking. And I know you don't want me to kiss you, so just stop. Please." He rubbed his face before fisting his hands at his sides, his eyes squeezed shut. "Please leave me alone."

My breath came in shallow little pants that stuck in my throat as I stepped forward and cupped his cheeks with my hands. "Who says I don't want you to kiss me?"

His eyes popped open, and I swooped down and pressed our lips together before I lost my nerve. It wasn't the hyper mashing it had been the first time at the pond, but I kissed him firmly. His lips were dry against mine, and this was probably a huge mistake, but as I tilted my head and softened the kiss with a gentle peck, I didn't care even a little.

Charlie's breath shuddered through him, and I nuzzled his cheek before drawing back, still holding his face. Snowflakes caught in his dark eyelashes, and he stared at me with parted lips. I caught a flake on my fingertip.

"But you're straight," he whispered hoarsely.

I shook my head, running my thumb over his lower lip, which was wet now.

"You have a girlfriend."

"We broke up after graduation. We're just friends now. She's dating guys in New York. I…well, I was going to come out at Stanford, but I haven't worked up the nerve. I know—super lame. You're the first guy I've ever kissed. I mean, obviously you were back then. But you are again now. First. And second."

He shook his head. "This isn't happening."

He tried to step back, but the snowbank was there, and he flailed for a moment as I grabbed his arms. "I know this must be a surprise, but—"

"A *surprise?*" He batted my hands away and edged around me to the open parking lot. The snow was coming harder now, the white flakes dotting his hair. "This is…what the fuck, Gavin? You were going to come out? What are you saying? You're bi now?"

"No. I'm gay. I've always been gay. I tried not to be. I tried to get over it. I tried so hard I became really good at denying it. Too good." My mouth was dry and the words were going to choke me, but I had to shove them out. "I'm sorry. I'm sorry for what I did. For how I stopped talking to you. I was afraid, but I know that's no excuse."

He shook his head. "I don't understand."

"I…at that party, after I danced with Candace and she made out with me, I tried to find you, but you'd already gone home. I threw rocks at your window, but you didn't come. I didn't want to be with her. I wanted you."

Charlie wrapped his arms around himself. "I saw you two together. I was really mad. Jealous."

"I'd have been pretty hurt too if the situation was reversed. The next morning, I went to talk to my dad. He was in the garage, working on the lawn mower. I told him what happened. Told him how much I liked you. That I wanted you to be my boyfriend."

I could still see it so clearly: the clumps of dried grass scattered on the grease-stained concrete floor, the cicadas humming in rising crescendos beyond the garage, and the driveway blacktop a little oozy in spots under the sun's merciless late-summer glare. Sweat had beaded on Dad's forehead, and it dripped down his temple as he stared at me.

"Kiddo, you're confused. This is normal. You're not gay. There's no way."

The jagged scars those words left still ached. Until he'd spoken them, I hadn't realized how much I'd needed him to tell me it was okay. That *I* was okay.

Charlie opened and closed his mouth. "You really liked me?" His voice was so small.

"More than anyone. I wanted to go kiss you again so bad. But my dad kept telling me it was a mistake. That I was confused, and the feelings would go away. That the move had been too stressful, and of course I'd gotten really attached to my first friend in Norwalk. He said I wasn't gay. That I couldn't be."

"And you believed him?" It was barely a whisper, Charlie's eyes shining.

I had to blink away my own tears. "He was my dad. He knew everything. He always knew the right things to do. I told myself he had to be right. He *had* to be. Because obviously he didn't want me to be gay. So I couldn't be. I had to stop."

Charlie gazed at me with such tenderness. "Gavin…"

I had to get it all out, so I barreled on. "The next day at school, when I saw you coming in the hall, I pretended I didn't. I walked right by you like you weren't there." I swiped at my cheeks. "I'm so sorry. I wish I could go back and do it differently. I wish I could have been stronger. But I didn't want to disappoint him. He told me not to tell my mom, and I just felt… God, I was so ashamed and afraid." I looked at the lights of the cars on the highway, trying to blink away my stupid tears.

I only realized Charlie had moved when I felt his cold hand grasp mine. "Why didn't you tell me?"

I forced myself to meet his gaze. "I wanted to. So much. But I knew I couldn't be friends with you and not need more. So I tried to pretend you weren't there. That Candace was everything I wanted. And I know you blamed her, but she's a good person. It wasn't her fault. She's actually the one that encouraged me to admit that I'm gay. She'd started to suspect, and she confronted me this summer. I was already working up my nerve to tell her, and she made it so much easier."

He nodded jerkily. "That's good."

"Back in ninth grade, I wanted to believe that if I didn't see you anymore, it would go away. Then I could be normal again. Then I wouldn't disappoint my dad and upset my mom. I was a coward, Charlie."

He squeezed so hard my fingers started to go numb. "You're really gay?"

I nodded. "I wanted to tell my parents before I left for college. But my dad has to know, and my mom's not stupid. I think they're hoping if we don't talk about it, it'll go away. Guess that's a Bloomberg family trait."

For a few heartbeats, Charlie just looked at me, and I tried to think of something else to say to explain why I'd been such a pathetic weakling. Then he was wrapping his arms around me so tight.

"It's okay, Gav. Everything will be okay."

As fresh tears burned my eyes, I bent my head to his shoulder and clung to him. "I'm sorry. I'm so sorry."

He petted my hair, murmuring little nothing words as the snow fell. It felt so good to have my arms around him, and when I lifted my head, our mouths came together like it was the only possibility. Our lips parted and Charlie's tongue slid against mine. I could taste the sweet-tart tang of Red Bull, and I wanted to keep kissing him and hearing the little moans he made low in his throat for days and days.

We pressed against each other the way we had years ago, but now we had muscles and stubble, and I'd never felt more like a *man* than I did in that parking lot in Ohio. "Please," I whispered.

He pulled back, his lips shiny and eyes dark. "You really want me, Gav?"

I groaned and thrust my hips against him. "I'll get down on my hands and knees right here."

Charlie kissed me again, sucking my tongue. We were both getting hard, and we rubbed against each other like dogs. He squeezed my ass. "I've dreamed about this for so long. Even when I hated you, I wanted to fuck you more than anyone else."

A wheezy *bang* echoed across the pavement to our dark corner, and we jumped apart, our chests heaving. We watched a pickup truck leave the parking lot, backfiring one more time before it disappeared toward the highway. Shit, fuck, *fuck*. My heart pounded and I exhaled, relief flooding through me.

Our eyes met, and we *laughed*, and God, it felt warm and sweet like hot chocolate to really laugh with Charlie again. I peered up at the thickening snow. "We should get back in the car."

We hurried across the parking lot. I looked down so I wouldn't slip on any icy patches, and my face hurt from smiling, my ears going numb in the cold.

I did it. I told him. I actually did it. And he actually kissed me back.

I had the keys, so I pressed the fob twice and got behind the wheel as Charlie went to the passenger side. A thin layer of fluffy snow covered the windshield and the back window, and was gathering on the side windows too. We sat there in silence for a few moments.

I cleared my throat. "Should we get some food? Then I guess we need a motel."

"Right. Uh-huh."

More silence. I remembered the whole Christmas/Ava situation, and reached over to cover Charlie's hand with my own. "Maybe the storm won't be as bad as they think. We might still make it."

Charlie squeezed his eyes shut, obvious guilt rippling through him. "Thank you." He opened his eyes again. "Thank you for letting me come along in the first place. I don't think I ever said that. I should have." He turned to me, and there was such tenderness in his gaze. "Thank you so much."

I leaned over and kissed him, and he opened his mouth, moaning softly as he grasped at me. I wanted to be naked with him— we had too many layers on and the gearshift was digging into my ribs. But God, *I was kissing Charlie Yates*. Wet, smacking sounds filled the confined space of the car, and I didn't even need to turn on the heat.

That summer, I'd been drawn to Charlie immediately—the way he'd raced straight into everything he did, seemingly without a moment's hesitation. But until he'd had the guts to kiss me by the pond, I hadn't been able to give my feelings a name. And as soon as I'd spoken them to my dad, I'd wished I could swallow them forever.

But I was done being quiet.

As my moan filled the car, Charlie tugged up my fleece and tried to unbutton my jeans, kissing my neck. The humid gusts of his breath sent shivers through me. "Need to touch you."

"Uh-huh," I agreed, letting go of his shoulders and back long enough to open my fly. My dick strained against my underwear, and I gasped when Charlie pulled it out with a cold touch. He stroked me, the friction sending sparks to my fingers and toes and little moans to my tongue.

Charlie has his hand on my cock.

"I dreamed about this so many times," I muttered, kissing him messily.

He didn't stop jerking me as he eyed me speculatively. "About being with a guy?"

"Yes," I panted. "But it was always you in my head."

Grabbing my face with his left hand, Charlie kissed me hard. He spit in his palm and then ran his thumb over the head of my cock, rubbing the drops there down over my shaft. I was on fire, but I wanted to touch him too. I fumbled at his jeans, whimpering at the loss as he let go of my dick to help me pull out his.

Then he was stroking me again, and I licked my palm and took hold of him. He wasn't cut, and I pulled down his foreskin. The angle was awkward, but I managed to get a good grip on him, and *holy crap I was touching a penis that wasn't mine. And it was Charlie's!* I figured I was doing okay by the way his breathing hitched.

"I dreamed of this too," he murmured, pressing our foreheads together. "Imagined what you'd look like when I made you come."

Groaning, I stroked him faster, the heat in my hand and in my groin flushing me all over. My heavy balls tightened. "Charlie…"

"Do you want to come for me?" He panted in puffs that mingled with mine as he stroked even faster. "That's it, Gav. Like that."

I spurted over his hand, shuddering and probably gripping his cock too tightly, but he didn't complain as I rode out the waves of my orgasm, my mouth open as he milked me. I closed my eyes and leaned against him, boneless but for the hand I still had wrapped around his dick.

"That's it," he repeated, letting go of me.

I opened my eyes to find him sucking my jizz off his fingers, and I was pretty sure I might come all over again. I got my second wind and concentrated on jerking him. "Your turn."

He buried his face in my neck and sucked hard as he thrust his hips into my grasp. It was too dark in the car with the snow thick on the windows, and I couldn't wait to get him in a room where I could see his cock and explore his foreskin. Take him in my mouth. "I want to taste your cum," I whispered.

Charlie thrust harder, grunting and fucking into my hand. "Yeah. Oh shit."

"I want to do everything with you."

With a sharp cry, he came, making my hand wonderfully sticky as he bit my neck lightly. He slumped against me, and I squeezed my hand out from between us. Tentatively, I licked my skin where his spunk had splattered me. It was salty and musky, and I took another taste.

"Plenty more where that came from," he said, raising his head with a smirk.

We kissed, and it tasted like sex. The few times with Candace, we'd cleaned up quickly, but I imagined with Charlie I could wallow in sweat and cum for days and love every second of it. "Before, did you compare wanting to kiss me to having the stomach flu?"

His laughter filled the car. "I guess I did. Um, sorry?"

I put on a solemn expression. "You make me want to vomit and shit my pants too."

Pressing a hand to his chest, Charlie shook his head. "That's the most romantic thing anyone has ever said to me."

We were laughing so hard we could barely kiss, but we found a way.

Six

Charlie

The motel was across from a strip mall with one of those drug stores that sells groceries, and Gavin volunteered to drive over and stock up on supplies after we secured our room. We'd gone by the drive-thru and scarfed down Big Macs and fries, and I was pleasantly sated from the food and sex.

I was also grinning to myself like a crazy person. I unlaced my sodden sneakers and left them at the door, being sure to shake as much snow out of my fleece as I could before spreading it over one of the two chairs by a little table in front of the window.

There were two queen beds, and my heart hopped, skipped, and jumped all over the place as I thought about being in one of those beds with Gavin. Of course the doubts were already whipping through my head. What if he changed his mind while he was across the street? Would he really want to have sex with me? Did he mean all that stuff he said?

"Enough!" My voice was sharp in the empty room. "Stop over-thinking this."

I cleaned the wheels of my pink suitcase with some toilet paper and heaved it up onto the closest bed. My hands shook as I brought my washing stuff into the bathroom and shut the door. Maybe I'd have a quick shower and clear my head. Scrub off the road stink.

My phone buzzed as I was climbing out of the tub and rubbing my wet skin with a cheap towel. "Hey, Mom. I was just about to call you."

"Where are you, honey? Another storm's moving in, and I really think you should stop for the night."

"Yeah. We got a motel room outside Sandusky." I hated saying it out loud, but there was no escaping it. "I'm not going to make it in time. I'm so sorry. Is she upset?"

Mom gave me one of her exasperated sighs. "Hon, there's not a reason in the world to be sorry. If there's one truth we can rely on, it's that there's not a darn thing we can do about the weather. Ava understands that. She's decided to postpone Christmas until you get back, so you boys take your time. There are pileups all over the place, and it's not worth the risk."

"Postpone Christmas?" My heart clenched. "What do you mean?"

"No presents or turkey until you're here. We'll just pretend the twenty-sixth is the twenty-fifth. Easy peasy."

"I don't want her to have to wait for presents."

"It's her choice, and that's that. Do you have enough money? Everything's going okay? Aside from the damn weather." She cleared her throat. "Darn weather, I should say."

I laughed. "I might need to borrow a little to pay off my credit card, but I can pay you back in the new year once I have more shifts at the library."

"Don't worry about that. We're covering your trip."

"But—"

"No buts. End of discussion. We're doing fine. I don't want you worrying about money. You worry about enough."

"I... Okay. Thanks."

"And Gavin's okay for money? I heard from Mrs. Papadakis that his parents are down south, so if he needs anything, we can help."

Stay casual. Be normal. "Gavin's okay. He's great. Everything's fine!" I cringed at my rushed, overly peppy tone. Ugh.

Mom was silent for a moment. "What's going on with Gavin?"

I bit back a groan. "Nothing, Mom. Is Ava there? I want to say hi."

"In a minute. Charlie, what aren't you telling me?"

It's not that I didn't want to tell her—she'd given great advice when I was dating Tim—but I was still processing everything. It hadn't even been an hour. But there was no point in trying to brush off my mom. "It's not bad. Turns out Gavin's gay too."

"Oh! So are you two…?"

"Maybe. I guess. I don't know what's going to happen." Questions whirled through my mind. *Is this just a holiday hookup? Are his parents going to freak out? How long does it take to get to Stanford from the city?* "I don't want to get ahead of myself."

"Right. I understand. But you know the drill, yes?"

"Yes, yes. Don't worry." Hmm. I actually hadn't packed condoms since I'd planned on spending all my time back home with Ava and my folks. Good thing that drugstore was across the street.

"I always worry, Charlie. It's my job. Hold on." Mom said to someone else, "Yes. Here you go."

Ava's little voice filled my ear. "Hi, Charlie. Are you okay?"

"Yeah, Bear. I'm fine." My eyes burned. Fuck, I missed her so much. "Stuck in this snow, though. But I don't want you to wait for me to have all your presents. You should have Christmas on the right day."

"No, I want to wait. It wouldn't be the same. I've never had a Christmas without you. It'll only be a day or two more. I've waited this long already. I'm good at waiting."

That nearly had me blubbering all over the place, but I kept it together. "I know you are. You don't think Santa will mind making two trips?"

She lowered her voice. "I'm sure he won't since he's actually Mom and Dad."

"Wait, what? That's crazy talk." She was eight now, but it still hit me with a pang that she didn't believe in Santa anymore.

"Going to every house in one night doesn't really seem possible. Besides, we don't have a chimney, and we lock the doors. It's okay, Charlie. I still love Christmas."

My throat tightened. "Me too, Bear. It'll be awesome. I'll try to make it home as soon as I can." I hated that I would miss Christmas Day, but I realized that the lingering terror of that nightmare had finally, finally evaporated. Listening to her talk now, I knew Ava was safe.

"I know. I can't wait to see you. But things are even better when you have to wait for them. Oh, guess what? Mom let me go skating today with Whitney and Nisha. It was so much fun! You won't believe what Nisha did."

As Ava rattled on, I was struck by how amazing it was that my baby sister was growing into this little person, with thoughts and ideas. There had been times I thought she'd never live to see eight years old, and I hoped with everything I had that the remission would hold. It was hard to breathe through the swell of pure affection.

"Sounds like a good day, Bear. Wish I'd been there." I'd managed to keep my voice steady, or so I thought.

"Don't cry, Charlie. I'll go skating with you when you get home. I promise."

"Yeah? Okay. It's a deal. Tell Mom I'll call in the morning. Love you, Bear. Give me a growl?"

She roared into the phone, and I roared back. After I hung up, there was a sharp rap on the door.

"Charlie? Are you okay?"

Laughing, I opened the door. "I'm fine. It was this thing Ava and I do. We shake, and we also roar. I know, we're freaking weird." I frowned. "Gavin?"

He was staring, and I realized I was naked. Gavin licked his lips, and I shamelessly trailed a hand down my chest to my cock, desire rushing through me. Before I could think of something porny to say, I noticed the colored lights behind him. "Wait, what?"

With a little smile, Gavin stepped aside. "I thought since you won't make it home on time, you could have a little Christmas here."

I walked into the room, taking in the strings of colored lights Gavin had hastily strung over the wide dresser, trailing them across the top of the TV. He'd done the same over the headboards on the beds. The overhead light was off, and the room glowed with color. On the table, a blue candle flickered. "Does Hanukkah start tonight?" I asked.

"Yeah. No menorahs at CVS. I figured the candle was better than nothing."

I stared some more. "It's..."

"Lame, I know. I can take it down."

Grabbing his arm, I shook my head. "Don't you dare. It's perfect." I pulled him into a hug, and it should have been weird since I was naked and he was in his jeans and sweatshirt, but it wasn't at all. I closed my eyes and breathed him in, all snowy and fresh and a little sweaty, and okay, he needed to be naked now too.

I started tugging and unzipping, and he stripped down in a blink. Jesus, he was gorgeous. Broad shoulders and slim hips, those long legs and lean muscles, and a curved, cut cock jutting up from a thatch of dark hair. His breathing was already shallow, and his gaze raked over me from top to bottom. I opened my mouth to ask him what he wanted, and Gavin sank to his knees.

Holy crap, my legs wobbled at the sight. The Christmas lights glowed pink, yellow, red, blue, and green, washing over his skin and making the auburn in his hair all the richer. I ran my fingers into it as he stared up at me with wide eyes and parted lips. He leaned into my touch as he ran his hands over my thighs. My cock was already hard.

Tentatively, he nuzzled against it, and I was so turned on I wouldn't have been surprised to see actual sparks flying off the end.

He licked his lips, still looking up at me, and it was all I could do not to thrust my hips and ram it into his mouth. His breath skated over my dick. He finally broke eye contact, circling the base with one hand and sucking the tip.

"Fuck!" My voice seemed too loud in the stillness of the room.

Gavin pulled off immediately and sat back on his heels with wide eyes. "Was that wrong?"

"Oh my God, no. Don't stop." I urged his head back, my patience unraveling in the face of my raging hard-on. "Please."

With a little smile and an apparent surge of confidence, Gavin not only kept going, but took it to the next level by opening his mouth wide and sucking me in as deep as he could. It was a good thing I had the wall beside the bathroom door to lean against, because I might have toppled over as his lips stretched around me, his nostrils flaring. Spit leaked from his mouth, and he licked and slurped, moving back and forth.

I was moaning and murmuring—"Oh, oh, fuck, Jesus, so good, yeah like that"—and Gavin seemed to like it, because the louder I got, the harder he sucked. My balls were so heavy, and I was pretty sure all the blood in my body was rushing to my crotch. I panted, my head spinning, as Gavin dug his fingers into my hips and took me in so deep he started to choke.

My hand was trembling, but I managed to smooth it over his head. "Not too much. It's okay. You're doing so good. Your mouth feels amazing."

He pulled off, coughing, and my dick slapped wetly against his chin. He was breathing hard and looking up at me, and I wanted to yank him to his feet to kiss him. But he went back to work on my cock, and it was hot and tight and *oh my God*. His eyes closed, and he swallowed me like he was starving for it, moaning low in his throat.

It didn't matter that he didn't have the smooth techniques of a couple of the guys I'd been with—God, this was so much better. This was *Gavin*. Gavin was actually doing this for me, and nothing had ever been so amazing in my whole life.

The wall was hard against my shoulder blades, and the carpet surprisingly soft under my feet. I dug in, making fists with my toes like in *Die Hard*. Panting and moaning, I caressed his head, my thighs trembling. I didn't want this to ever end, but I couldn't last.

My balls drew up. "So close." I urged him back in case he didn't want to swallow, and he stared up at me with glazed eyes. I jerked myself hard and came on his face and neck, and it was better than I'd ever imagined. It splashed white on his skin, so warm in the glow of the colored lights.

I moaned, milking myself and twitching with each drop, watching it drip down as I marked him. There was a string of it over his bottom lip and chin, and his pink tongue darted out to swipe it up. "Fuck, Gavin," I muttered, brushing my fingers over his cheek.

I pulled him to his feet and shoved my tongue in his mouth. He pressed me back hard against the wall, bending down to kiss me as he humped against my hip. He was rock hard, and I wanted to tell him I'd suck him off, but I couldn't seem to do anything but lick into his mouth, tasting a hint of my own spunk there and groaning. My dick was sensitive and it hurt as he shoved against me, but I didn't give a shit. I tried to hook a leg up over his hip, but he was too tall, and I just wrapped my arms around him.

"Come on. Yeah, that's it," I muttered as he rutted against me.

Gavin shoved his face against my neck, panting wetly as he shuddered and came hot and sticky, his cock trapped between us. We stood slumped there, and I rubbed his back, running my fingers up and down his spine. Sweat dampened the hair at his neck.

He kissed the chicken pox scar behind my ear, sending a fresh shiver of want through me. "I wanted to do that since that summer by the pond," he whispered. "Wanted to suck cock."

Nuzzling his shoulder, I said, "You're a natural."

He lifted his head then, his gaze intent. "Wanted to suck *your* cock, Charlie."

I took his face in my hands and kissed him again, trying not to think about how different high school would have been. All the things we could have done. Not just sex, but…everything.

We had a long shower together, kissing and touching and not saying much. When we were dried off and stretched out on the bed closest to the bathroom, the covers pushed down to our feet, Gavin rolled onto his side and propped his head on his hand.

"Is Ava upset about Christmas?"

"She's actually handling it really well. Says we'll just postpone everything until I get there. Presents, turkey—all of it. I'm insanely lucky to have her for a sister. She's more mature at eight than I'll ever be."

Gavin ran his palm over my chest, teasing the hair there and sending lazy pleasure through me like honey. "I can't imagine what she's been through."

"Yeah. It's been tough." *Tough* didn't really begin to describe it, but if I said more I'd probably get upset. Instead, I rolled onto my side facing Gavin. The colored lights danced over his skin, and I still couldn't believe this was real life. I ran my finger over his lips and kissed him. "Hi."

"Hey," he mumbled, sliding his big thigh between mine. I tried to think of something clever or witty to say, but then Gavin asked, "Will you fuck me?" He seemed to hold his breath as the words escaped his lips.

My balls tightened at the mere thought. "Is that a trick question?"

He laughed, a blush flooding his cheeks. "I was afraid you wouldn't want to. I mean, I won't be very good. I'm sure you're used to…"

I raised an eyebrow. "I don't think I'm as much of an expert as you seem to believe."

His forehead creased. "But you had that boyfriend. And you've hooked up at college, right?"

"Sure, but none of that matters." I gently pushed him onto his back and straddled his hips, my hands on his chest so I could caress his nipples and see him gasp. The urge to *touch, touch, touch* was overwhelming now that I actually could. I mean, I was in a *motel room* with *Gavin*, and we were having sex. All kinds of sex. This was so many sticky fantasies come to life, and the greatest Christmas present ever.

The guilt of not making it back in time for Ava flashed through me like a bullet, but I reasoned that *not* having sex while being snowbound wouldn't change anything.

"Well, it's safe to say you've done more than me." Gavin ran his hands up and down my thighs, sending sparks through me.

"It's also safe to say that this is the greatest sex I've ever had."

His brows drew together. "But..."

Leaning over, I pressed a slow kiss to his mouth. "Because it's you, Gav. It's different with you."

"God, Charlie. I want you so much. All this time... I'm sorry I—"

I kissed him and sat up. "It doesn't matter. We're here now. That's what counts. Are you sure you want to go all the way? It can hurt. Especially at first."

"Have you done it? Been on the bottom, I mean?"

"Uh-huh. I've liked it sometimes. If you want to top me, you can." The thought of Gavin inside me rocketed a thrill down my spine.

"I..." He bit his lip. "I want to. I want to do everything with you. But is it okay if you do it to me first? It's been my..." He swallowed hard.

My breath came faster. "Your what?" Rolling my hips against him, I leaned over again and licked his nipples and up to his neck. "Tell me."

Gavin shuddered. "It's been my biggest fantasy. Being...being fucked." He flushed. "Is that weird?"

"If by weird, you mean so hot I might come all over you at the thought." I kissed him, sliding our tongues together until we were both panting. "You want my cock in you?"

"Yes, yes, yes. Do it, Charlie. I bought stuff at the drugstore. In the bag on the table."

I groaned as I broke away. "Don't move."

When I turned back to the bed, Gavin was waiting just where I'd left him, and his dick curved up to his stomach as he stroked it lightly. The lights sent shimmers over him, and if I didn't have an ironclad rule against naked pictures—because once that shit is in the cloud it is never coming out—I would have happily taken about a hundred photos.

But I was also pretty keen to fuck him, so I crawled onto the mattress. "You still sure about this? It's gonna hurt." *Please say yes. Please say yes.*

"Yes. It might not hurt that much. I've been…" The blush was back, and his gaze skittered away. "I've been…you know."

I sat back on my heels beside him and ripped open the packet of lube. "You have to give me a little more to go on."

With an embarrassed huff, Gavin confessed, "I bought a dildo."

The mental images exploded in my cerebral cortex, and I was speechless, my heart thumping.

He turned his head away. "I know. It's lame, right?"

"I don't think that word means what you think it means. Because that is incredibly hot."

Looking at me again, Gavin bit his lip. "Really?"

My throat was dry. "What kind is it?"

An uncertain smile lifted Gavin's lips, as if he couldn't tell if I was joking or not. "Rubber."

"How many inches?"

"Six."

Lube was dripping over my fingers, and I nudged Gavin's knee with mine. "Spread your legs for me." With a shaky inhalation, he did, and I scooted between them, holding up my slick fingers. "Lift your ass a little." Gavin did as he was told, and reached down to spread his cheeks. Holy shit, I thought I would come right there. The trust in his eyes as he opened himself for me made my cock throb and something warm in my chest bloom. I ran my slippery index finger over his hole, and his breath caught.

"Charlie," he whispered.

I teased the rim of his hole. "Where did you buy it?"

"Huh?"

"The dildo."

"A sex shop in the Castro. It took me a month to work up the nerve to go in."

I wanted to simultaneously cuddle him and fuck his brains out. "How do you do it?" I pushed my finger a tiny bit inside. "How do you use it?"

"I…" His brow furrowed.

"I mean, do you get on your hands and knees? Or laying down like this?" I worked my finger in deeper.

He gasped. "Charlie, please. Give me more."

"You can take it, huh?" I made sure my middle finger was lubed up before pushing it in. "You like that?"

"Oh, yes." His hands trembled where he held himself open. "I love it. I…" He took a deep breath, and then the words tumbled out. "I fuck myself like this, and all the ways I can think of. It feels so good."

I worked him with my fingers now, in and out. "One day I want to watch you fuck yourself, and I'm going to jerk off all over you while you do it." I practically blushed at my own words. I'd never said much at all during sex, but Gavin apparently brought it out in me. It was dangerous to talk about *one day*, but the words kept coming. "I'm going to fuck your mouth while you're rammed full with the dildo, and you're going to come so hard."

"Yes! Please, Charlie." He squeezed around my fingers. "Need you now. Need more."

My cock was aching already, and when I eased out my fingers to roll on the condom, I had to take some deep breaths and think about math equations. An idea popped into my head. "Get up. Let me lie down." Gavin leapt straight up, and we both laughed as I stretched out and tugged his hips until he was straddling me. "You can control it better this way. And I can watch you."

His chest rising and falling rapidly, Gavin nodded jerkily and reached back for my cock. "This is good." He lifted up on his knees and then sank down, the head of my cock nudging at him. He groaned.

"Do you use the dildo like this? Do you sit on it?" The thought of Gavin in his dorm room fucking himself made me flush all over.

"Uh-huh." His thighs flexed as he pushed down. "But you feel so much better. Oh, Charlie." Wincing, he sank more, and we both moaned loudly as he slowly took me inch by inch. He was sweating, lowering himself and stretching his ass around me.

It was like fire in the best way, and he was so tight my eyes rolled back in my head. My toes twitched, and I had to get hold of myself. I was not going to blow my load a minute into Gavin's first time. And holy shit, the knowledge that my dick was the first one to ever be inside him and feel this made me dizzy with joy. Sex in the past had been about getting off and having fun, but this was so much more.

"Charlie." Gavin rose up a few inches and sank back down. "God, it's…you're so big."

I wasn't really—just over six inches long—but I was thick. I lifted my hips, not too hard, and thrust up into him. "You're so tight. Jesus, Gav." Eyes flashing, he groaned, starting to fuck himself in earnest now. I caressed his thighs. "That's it."

We both panted, and watching Gavin ride my cock was so exquisitely good that I could have done it for hours if I could have held off my orgasm long enough. Gavin's mouth was open, and his head tipped back as he lifted up and down, taking me deep. I wanted to lick the long line of his throat, but settled for touching his chest and everywhere I could reach besides his cock, which bounced along.

Gavin cried out, "Oh!" His head snapped up and he leaned onto me, his hands on my shoulders. "God, that feels…" He gasped, squirming on my dick.

"That's it. Did you find the spot? That's it, Gav. Come on."

He stared at me, his breath puffing against my face as he fucked himself. "I can't believe we're doing this."

"Me either."

We laughed, and Gavin kissed me messily, our tongues and teeth clashing. He was grunting now, slamming himself down harder than I would have dared fuck him the first time. His brow glistened with sweat, and I thought my cock would possibly explode when I came. The pleasure radiated out from my groin, flames of it licking over my body. It wasn't going to be long now, but Gavin had to finish first.

I took hold of his leaking cock and stroked it roughly, smearing the liquid around and rubbing hard. "Look at me."

Gavin did, his unfocused gaze snapping to mine, the grunts and groans still escaping his parted lips. "Charlie," he moaned.

"I want to watch you come."

He nodded. "Almost. Charlie, it's…close…please…"

Straining and panting, he rode me while I stroked him, and my heartbeat thundered in my ears as he jerked and came, spurting all over me. He clamped down on my cock, and it was so tight. I fucked up into him until I let go and closed my eyes, crying out. The sweet burn rushed through me in waves before fading.

Gasping, Gavin collapsed onto me, his breath hot on my neck. We were a sweaty, sticky mess, and I never, ever wanted it to end.

Seven

Gavin

December 24th

I had sex with a guy.

Not just any guy, of course. We'd mostly dozed the past few hours, and now it was after midnight. I was stretched out on my back, and beside me on his belly, his leg hooked over mine, Charlie slept with lips parted, his cheek smushed into the pillow he held. It was sweaty where our legs touched, but I wasn't moving. No way, Jose.

We'd pulled the covers up, and with the soft, colored glow of the Christmas lights, it was like being in a cozy little oasis.

My Hanukkah candle guttered on the table, melted almost all the way down into the cheap glass holder. At home, we'd have lit the *shamash* candle in the middle of the menorah, and the first candle on the right. We never went to synagogue, but we still followed a few traditions, even if it was half assed.

I chuckled as I remembered my mom grumbling through Yom Kippur.

"Can't we atone and still have our coffee? The ancient Jews didn't have to sit through an HR presentation without caffeine. And the donuts were right in front of me! It was cruel. I don't think the big boss upstairs minded that I had a Boston cream. It was another thing to atone for."

"What?" Charlie mumbled.

"Nothing. Just thinking."

He blinked sleepily. "About what?"

"Bunch of stuff." I trailed the back of my hand over his arm. "You know, I always wished I could have a Christmas tree. I love the lights and everything."

"Maybe it's because I'm a heathen, but I don't see why you can't. It's not like Santa and Rudolph and all that shit was in the Bible. It's not a religious holiday for everyone. Santa is nondenominational."

I chuckled. "That's true." It was on the tip of my tongue to say that next year we could have a menorah and a tree, but luckily I stopped myself. Because whoa, that was crazy, thinking about next year as if we were some *couple*, and as if we'd be living together or something. I was getting epically ahead of myself. I'd only just had gay sex for the first time.

Wow. It hit me again—I'd actually had sex with a guy.

Charlie rubbed his leg over mine. "Tell me."

"I feel like—" I broke off. It was too dumb to say out loud. But Charlie just waited, watching me patiently, so I spit it out. "I feel like I lost my virginity, and I should get some official recognition that I'm gay. Like a membership card or something."

"It'll be in the mail. Might take a few extra days to process, what with the holidays."

I nodded. "Oh, good to know. Is it laminated and everything?"

"Yep. You'll need it to get into clubs and stuff. Make sure you don't lose it. The American Association of Queers doesn't like issuing cards twice. They'll charge you a replacement fee."

"It's only fair."

We smiled, and Charlie rubbed his palm over my chest, still splayed on his stomach. "But you weren't a virgin, right?"

"No. With Candace, I…we only did it a few times. We waited a long time, which was fine with me, of course. I left it all up to her. But I guess I was a gay virgin, which isn't even really a thing."

"Sure it is." He plucked gently at my chest hair. "Why didn't you go cruising in San Fran? Man, when you went to the Castro to buy that dildo, you could have found dozens of guys to plug you."

Didn't want dozens of guys. Just you.

"I was nervous. With Candace, I wasn't intimidated. I knew her so well, and it was awkward and kind of weird, but it didn't scare me. Being with some guy I didn't know was just…I guess I wasn't ready. I was afraid I'd do it all wrong. So I bought the toy and figured I'd practice."

"Practice clearly makes perfect." He tweaked my nipple, sending a ripple of pleasure through me.

"Yeah?" I knew I was blushing. "Um, thanks. You too." Although I didn't want to think about how many guys Charlie had practiced with. It was totally unfair, but jealousy simmered in my gut. "I went to the Castro a few times to walk around, and I wondered if I'd see you there." I scoffed. "As if all gay people in San Fran just hang out constantly in the Castro, right?"

Charlie watched me carefully, his hand still, resting on my sternum. "But you hated me."

"Well, I did, but I didn't really. I was angry with you after the pizzeria incident. It was…it made it all easier if I let myself pretend that you were an asshole and none of it was my fault. But you were always the one I thought about when I jerked off. God, I still wanted you."

He seemed to take this in while drawing little circles on my skin with his thumb. "Really?"

"I tried so hard not to. When Mrs. Papadakis from down the street told me you were going to San Fran too, I couldn't believe it. I didn't know what to think. I was mad at you, but after what I did in ninth grade…" My throat was dry. "I'm so sorry."

"I know. It sucked, but it's done now. Who knows what would have happened if you'd waited for me on the first day of school. Maybe we would have gotten together and crashed and burned by Halloween."

I thought back to that day, and how early I'd gotten showered and dressed so I could walk the half mile to school alone. "You still wanted to go with me, even after the party? When I threw rocks at your window that night, you didn't answer."

Sighing, he closed his eyes. "By Tuesday, I'd decided it was okay. If you were straight, at least we could still be friends. That was the most important thing."

Ugh. The guilt razored through me, and I picked up his hand and kissed his palm, not having a clue what to say.

"I knocked on your door, and your mom answered. Said you'd left already. I felt like puking all over her rosebushes, but I still thought I'd be able to find you at school, and we'd pretend it had never happened. The whole way there, I rehearsed what I'd say to you, and how casual and cool I'd be. But then when you walked right by me in the hall like I didn't even exist…"

"I'm sorry," I whispered. "I'd give anything to change it." I inched closer and kissed his shoulder.

He opened his eyes. "I'm sorry too. We can't change the shit we did." He kissed me tenderly, only a brush of lips. We breathed each other in, pressing our foreheads together wordlessly.

When Charlie pulled back, he kissed the tip of my nose. "Let's get back to you fantasizing about me while jerking off. This needs further exploration."

I laughed, the pressure in my chest relieving. "I'm sure you can connect the dots."

"I do have a vivid imagination, but I want details, Bloomberg. Spill."

"Well, I'd watch a video or think about some hot actor. But in the end, it was always you, or else I couldn't…"

Charlie pressed closer against my side, propping his head on his hand. His dick brushed my hip. "You couldn't get off unless you imagined me?"

If I hadn't been blushing before, I sure was now. But it was the truth, so I nodded and looked away.

Running his hand up my chest, Charlie tipped my head toward him with a finger on my chin. I wasn't sure what to expect, but he wasn't laughing at me. His eyes were dark, and he leaned down and kissed me, licking into my mouth. When he pulled back, he traced his hand down my body again, this time circling it around my cock, which woke up in a hurry.

"What did you think about?"

"You know…stuff." My breath stuttered as he played with the head of my dick.

"Hmm, stuff." He smiled wickedly. "You'll have to be more specific." He nudged my legs farther apart and reached down to skim his fingertip over my hole. "Did you think about my cock in your ass?"

"Uh-huh." It was tender, but I loved the sensation of his finger teasing me. I blurted, "When I watched porn, I'd think about you in all the positions."

"Yeah?" He rubbed his thickening dick against my hip. "Sucking you? Fucking you? What about fucking me?"

I nodded so hard I almost banged my head on the bed frame.

Charlie licked his palm and stroked my cock again. "How did you have me? On my back? Side?"

"Sometimes. But usually…"

"On my stomach? Hmm, or maybe on my hands and knees?"

My cock jumped in his hand and I moaned.

Smiling slyly, he kissed me messily, all spit and tongue as he kept working my dick. "Doggy style, with you behind me? You're bigger, so you could really *take* me. Ram your cock into me. Give it to me until I screamed your name."

I grabbed his head, pulling on his hair to yank him into a kiss while I thrust into the grip of his hand. "Yes," I moaned.

Charlie tore himself away, but he was back in a second, tossing the condoms at me before turning onto his hands and knees. "Do it. Fuck, please." He squeezed lube onto his fingers and reached back to his ass.

I dropped the condom packet three times before I was able to rip it open and roll it over my cock. I watched him grease his hole, shoving his fingers inside, and had to squeeze the base of my shaft to get in control. Crawling behind him, I took hold of his wrist, easing his fingers out and going up on my knees. The sheet was bunched under me and I pulled it free.

His hole glistened, and I spread his ass open. I probably would have stared at it for an hour if he'd let me, but he jerked his butt back.

"Come on, Gavin. Fuck me the way you've always wanted to."

It took two tries to get my cock inside him, the head shoving against his ring of tight muscle. I didn't want to hurt him, and I pushed experimentally. No movement. I tried again, and Charlie groaned.

"Dude, ram it in there. I won't break. I promise. It's okay if it hurts. It's part of it."

He was right, of course—the burn had made the pleasure all the more intense when I'd impaled myself on his cock. Gripping his hips, I thrust into him, stretching his tight hole around me as I inched inside. With another shove, I went all the way, my hips slamming into his ass. We both cried out, and I hoped our neighbors weren't light sleepers.

If they were, sucked to be them, because I moaned and grunted and shouted as I fucked Charlie hard. He took everything I gave him with his own pants and cries, and the sound of our flesh slapping together filled the room. Grabbing his shoulder with one hand, I leaned over him and went even deeper.

He was so hot, squeezing around me, and I loved how hard I could go. I didn't have to worry about being too heavy, and his low groans were just like I'd imagined them. He was spread open for me so perfectly, and I wanted to fuck him all night. I hoped I was doing it right. But God, the fact that I was doing it at all was everything. Our skin was slick where we pressed together, and I breathed through my mouth, trying to find a rhythm.

"Oh yeah," Charlie moaned. "There. Hit that again. Fuck me good."

He sounded like the people in pornos, and I *loved* it. My blood ran so hot there was probably steam coming out of my ears as I pounded him. He was super tight, and I wished I could come inside him. I wanted to fill him up until it dripped out, assuming that was actually possible.

My leg was cramping, and my balls were super tight, so I reached around for his cock, pumping him hard.

When he came, he shouted so loudly the people at the twenty-four-hour drug store across the street probably heard it. He squeezed hard with his ass, and I kept thrusting, tangling one hand in his sweaty hair as I pushed to the finish line. I closed my eyes, still seeing colored explosions of light, my orgasm shuddering through me.

Panting, we tumbled into a sweaty pile. Charlie took hold of my hand and kissed it. "Your membership card is definitely in the mail."

I had to get rid of the condom and clean up, but I stayed splayed over his back for a little bit longer, smiling against his skin.

Charlie

"Charlie!"

I bolted up as Gavin and the cheap motel room came into focus. Gavin was kneeling beside me on the bed with the glow of his phone lighting his face and the fairy lights a rainbow beyond him. "What?" I cleared my throat, coughing. "What happened?" I blinked at the clock beside the bed. One-fifteen p.m.

"It's a full-on Christmas miracle. The storm went north. The roads east of here aren't bad. If we leave now and drive all night we can make it for the twenty-fifth! You can be there when Ava wakes up!"

I was wide awake now, adrenaline surging through my veins. "Are you serious?"

Gavin tilted his head and drew his brows together. "No, I'm messing with you. Psych! Hilarious joke." He slapped my shoulder and bounded off the bed. "Let's go!"

I jumped up after him and went for my clothes, but then I looked down at the jizz dried in my chest hair. "Shit. I'd better have a quick shower."

"I'm way ahead of you," Gavin called from the bathroom. The sound of water followed. "Give me a few minutes. Faster if we do it separately."

"Do you really think we can make it?" I called. I was afraid to get my hopes up, but they were soaring.

"What?"

"Nothing!" I unzipped my suitcase and took out clean clothes before shoving everything else back in. After unplugging the Christmas lights, I squeezed them in too.

When he came out of the bathroom dripping, rubbing a towel over his hair, I took a split second to appreciate how freaking *gorgeous* my boyfriend was. *Whoa.* The thought had popped into my head so naturally. But was he my boyfriend now? I was probably seriously jumping the gun.

But did he want to be? What if—

OH MY GOD, GET YOUR ASS IN THE SHOWER AND FRET OVER YOUR RELATIONSHIP STATUS LATER.

I scurried to follow my inner drill sergeant's command, closing the bathroom door behind me so I could take a dump, because it was definitely too early in whatever this was to drop a deuce with the door open. Call me old fashioned.

I soon climbed into the shower, where I squeezed out the last of the motel shampoo and conditioner, and scrubbed myself down. I realized I was grinning, and I hummed "Jingle Bells." Soon we'd be dashing through the snow, and I'd get to see my Ava's perfect little face on Christmas morning. As I hopped out, I sung to myself.

"Over the fields we go, laughing all the way. Bells on bobtail ring—" I wondered what the hell a bobtail was, and put my hand on the doorknob to go ask Gavin when I realized he was talking to someone on the phone.

"Yeah, Dad. It's been great, actually. Not what I expected at all."

I smiled to myself. It had been rather great, hadn't it?

"No, you know I don't mind my alone time. I've been catching up on my reading. I'd better go. Glad you and Mom are having a good time. Have fun paddle boarding!"

Standing there on the tiles, naked and wet, I forced in a breath. It was like I'd been sucker punched right in the face (not to mention the nads), and I supposed Gavin did owe me one. So, apparently boyfriend status was definitely premature. Good to know. I tried to focus. *There are valid reasons for not telling his dad right now. He's not even out yet. It's cool. Don't spaz. It doesn't mean anything.*

But shit, man. Did it hurt.

I dried off in a rush, and didn't look at him as I hustled into my clothes. Everything was fine. I'd just have to see what happened. No sense in making a scene, especially since it wasn't as if we'd exchanged promise rings. Before a few days ago, we hadn't even spoken in years. What did I expect? It was no big deal.

"Charlie? You okay?"

"Uh-huh," I lied. "Just anxious about getting home. Now that it's a possibility again, I really want to make it."

"I know. We will." With his dimpling cheeks and kind eyes, he took my face in his hands and kissed me tenderly. "I'm going to get you there on time. Okay?"

96

I could have stayed there forever in that moment kissing him, but I nodded. I couldn't let myself worry about the future. Gavin was here with me now, and we were on the move, because Christmas couldn't wait.

Eight

Gavin

December 25th

It was just past one in the morning when we pulled into the Yates' driveway. Charlie killed the engine, and we looked at each other. "We actually made it for Christmas morning," I said. It had been a slow drive out of Sandusky, but the plows had been out in force once we'd reached Pennsylvania.

Charlie stared at his house, which shone with Christmas lights strung across the roof and on the bushes along the front window, which glowed a warm yellow. He grinned. "Come on."

"Oh, are you sure? I can just…" I motioned up the street to where my dark house stood.

"You don't want to come in?"

"No, I do—I just don't want to intrude."

He rolled his eyes. "I wouldn't be here if it wasn't for you. You're not intruding." He climbed out and shut the door quietly, and I followed suit, relieved. It would have been fine to go home—I certainly missed my bed. But it wasn't nearly as inviting as the Yates' house, with warmth spilling from it as Mrs. Yates opened the door and hauled Charlie into a hug. I hung back on the stoop as she took his face in her small hands and kissed his forehead, chin, cheeks, and nose. She was blonde and petite, and pretty in that comforting mom way.

Charlie's parents both wore robes over their pajamas, and Mr. Yates edged past his wife to extend his hand to me. He was tall, paunchy, and balding, but had Charlie's killer smile.

"Gavin, so nice to see you," he said quietly. "Thank you for making sure Charlie made it home. Please come in. Are you hungry? Thirsty?"

Smiling, I shook his hand and closed the door behind me. "It was my pleasure, sir." Of course then my cheeks got incredibly hot, and I stammered and concentrated on untying my sneakers. But Mr. Yates didn't seem to notice, and he yanked Charlie into a big hug. As they spoke quietly, Mrs. Yates took my coat.

She asked me, "How about some hot chocolate?"

"That would be great, but I probably shouldn't stay long. It's so late. Or early, depending on your perspective."

"I was thinking Gavin could stay until he goes skiing tomorrow," Charlie said.

"Oh, of course!" Mrs. Yates was still whispering. "We'd love to have you. We don't want you going home alone." A *thump-thump-thump-thump* from above had her sighing. "I guess the jig is up."

Charlie raised his eyebrows. "Did you seriously think she was going to sleep through the night? You're such an optimist, Mom." He jumped onto the bottom of the staircase, shouting, "Because this bear is out of hibernation, isn't she?"

A remarkably loud growl accompanied the blur of movement that was Ava barreling down the stairs into Charlie's arms. He gave her a roar, and she wrapped herself around him. She was still small for eight, which made sense after how sick she'd been.

Her hair was growing back into brown almost-curls that reached her ears, and she was possibly the most adorable thing I'd ever seen, especially in Charlie's arms. He squeezed her with an expression of such tenderness and love that my eyes burned watching them.

Mrs. Yates looked ready to cry herself, and her husband wrapped an arm around her shoulders. Ava dropped down to her feet and spun to where I stood off to the side.

"Hi, Gavin! I don't know if you remember me."

"I sure do." I smiled. "It's really nice to meet you again."

She came to me and threw her arms around my waist. "Thank you for bringing Charlie home for Christmas."

"Of course." I patted her head and hugged her back.

"It was meant to be, the way that storm moved north," Mr. Yates said. "I think Santa pulled a few strings for that miracle."

Ava bounced on her toes. "Did he come yet?"

Mrs. Yates brushed a hand over Ava's hair. "He just might have, but you know you have to wait until Christmas morning."

"It *is* Christmas morning! It's past midnight."

Charlie slung his arm around her. "How about we open our stockings now? Since Mom and Dad are already up, we won't have to wake them at five or six."

"He raises an excellent point," Mr. Yates said.

Mrs. Yates smiled. "I'll put on the kettle for hot chocolate, and I suppose we'd better check the mantel."

Ava tore off down the hall, and I followed the family past the kitchen to the den. That summer I moved to Norwalk, I'd spent so many days in this house, and especially in the den. The thick beige carpet and sectional couch was the same, as was the brick fireplace and wood accents around the windowless room. The huge TV over the mantel was new, and I imagined how awesome it would be playing video games on it. Maybe Charlie and I could have some rematches.

We're friends again, but are we definitely more than that? What's going to happen after Christmas?

Ava squealed as she took in the brightly wrapped gifts tumbling out from beneath the Christmas tree in the corner. "There are so many!"

"Guess you're on the nice list this year, huh?" Charlie asked. "Unless those are all for me."

"I believe Mom and Dad rated a few presents too," Mrs. Yates commented.

Charlie shrugged. "I *guess.*"

Giggling, Ava eyed the bulging stockings hanging from the mantle. "Can we, can we?"

"I suppose we can," Mr. Yates said with a broad smile.

I perched on the couch beside Charlie's parents while Charlie and Ava flopped down on the carpet and went to town on their stockings, oohing and ahhing over the little gifts squeezed inside. I assumed Mrs. Yates had done all the shopping, and they all had toiletries in their stockings, as well as toys for Ava and a new race car video game for Charlie.

With a furrow in her brow, Mrs. Yates unwrapped the tissue from a small bottle in her stocking. She gasped softly, beaming at her husband. "Chanel. How did this get in here?"

"Hey, ask Santa. I wouldn't know." He kissed her and continued emptying his own stocking.

"Oh!" Mrs. Yates went to the mantel and picked up a white envelope. "Gavin, here's a little something for you."

"What? You didn't have to do that." I took the envelope, staring at my name written in gracefully swooping letters.

Mrs. Yates sat beside me again and gave my arm a squeeze. "It's just a little thank you."

I opened the envelope and pulled out the blue and silver Hanukkah card, decorated with snowflakes and little stars of David. When I opened it, a hundred dollar iTunes gift card plopped onto my lap. "Wow. Thank you so much! You really didn't have to."

"It was Hanukkah Harry," Mr. Yates assured me. "He stopped by just before Santa."

Chuckling, I read the card.

Warmth of joy, glow of prosperity, sparkle of happiness.

May you be blessed with all these things and more.

In her neat script, Mrs. Yates had added:

Thank you for being such a good friend to Charlie. We hope to see more of you!

Love,

Maria, Graham, and Ava

"Thank you." I managed to keep my smile in place, even though I wanted to protest that I was a fraud. That I hadn't been a good friend at all to Charlie, not even after Ava got sick, when I should have put my own fears aside.

But as I looked around at the Yates family, opening their stockings in the middle of the night, I realized it wasn't about me. Charlie was right that we couldn't change the past, and no matter what happened between us, I'd do everything I could now to be the friend they thought I was.

It was the middle of the night, and I should have been exhausted. And I was, but my eyes didn't want to close. Wired and restless, I stared at the ceiling of the guest room. Charlie was across the hall, and I itched to tiptoe over and see if he was sleeping. He probably was. Probably out like a light.

I closed my eyes resolutely. Time to sleep now. We'd be up again in a few more hours for Christmas morning, so I needed to rest. Inhaling and exhaling, I counted out my breaths, making them longer and longer. *That's it. Getting sleepy. Time to drift away.*

With a sigh, I opened my eyes and turned over, sprawling out on the queen-sized bed. Then I tried the other side. Then my belly. Then on my back again. My blood pressure rose as I kicked off the covers. *Sleep, damn it! GO TO SLEEP!*

My breath caught as the door squeaked open a crack. I blinked in the darkness, reaching up to pull back one of the curtains by the bed. The moonlight flooding in illuminated Charlie shutting the door behind him. Grinning, he climbed into bed and right on top of me. I loved his weight, the rightness of it warming me like the steady glow of a candle. I opened my mouth for his tongue.

We both wore T-shirts and flannel pajama bottoms, and I stole under Charlie's hem, touching the lean muscles of his back. Opening my legs, I moaned into Charlie's mouth as he fit between my thighs and rocked his hips against mine. I wanted to get naked and throw my legs up to my ears so Charlie could fuck my ass. The thought of him pounding me had my balls tingling.

Or maybe he could ride my cock the way I had his. I would love to be inside him. But there was no way I'd be able to keep quiet. Kissing him roughly, I rutted desperately.

Breaking the kiss, Charlie pushed himself up on one hand and sucked my earlobe. His whisper sent icy-hot shivers through me. "What do you want?"

Not able to speak actual words, I grabbed his ass and ground our cocks together through too many layers of flannel and cotton.

"I really want to fuck you again, but we can't here." He thrust his hips, panting in my ear. "But maybe you want me to suck you?"

I actually bit my tongue hard enough to make my eyes water. Nodding hard, I pulled at his clothes, but he crawled back out of reach, yanking down my boxers and PJ bottoms. My tee got hung up on my arm, but I managed to tug it free and toss it onto the floor. I was naked and Charlie wasn't, and for some reason that made my cock stiffen even more.

He sat back on his heels by my feet, and he seemed to be waiting. A flush swept up my neck to my cheeks, which was silly since he'd seen me naked before. But whispering together here in the quiet hours in the silver-snowy moon glow, it was all the more intimate. With a deep breath, I spread my legs, bending my knees and taking them as wide open as I could.

Charlie's breath stuttered, and he licked his lips and nodded. He took his time, running his palms over my shins and nuzzling my inner thighs, the rough rub of his stubble making me gasp. My cock curved up to my belly, and I reached for it. Charlie grabbed my wrist and shook his head, pressing both my hands up by my head.

I was so exposed, but I knew I was safe with Charlie. Even when he was saying and doing dirty things, there was always a gentleness beneath it all. I'd finally revealed the deep, dark real me—the man that even Candace never knew. I wasn't a boy anymore, and I trusted Charlie completely with my truth.

His teasing kisses and touches feathered over my chest. I whimpered while he sucked each of my nipples into hard nubs, all of his concentration seemingly on giving me the greatest amount of pleasure he could. I tried to reach for him again, but he *tsked* and gently kissed each of my palms before pressing my arms up.

As he licked into my bellybutton, I threaded my fingers into his hair, needing to touch. My dick strained, and I arched my hips, trying to rub the shaft against him. The puff of his chuckle tickled my skin.

"Please," I whispered.

Charlie sat back on his heels and stroked my parted thighs, watching me with a half smile. When he leaned forward again, I exhaled the breath I'd been holding, certain he was finally going to put me out of my sweet misery. But his mouth found my ear again.

"You're such a slut for it, aren't you?" I imagined that with most guys, the question would have been rough and crude, but with Charlie, it was a loving whisper, like he could see right into me and wanted to draw me out with no judgment.

Gasping, I nodded vigorously, my gut tightening with sticky desire. I *was* a slut for it, and Charlie made me feel so good about it. Maybe it was weird to be turned on by that—to be touched by that—but I was.

"A slut for *me*, aren't you, Gavin?" He nipped my earlobe.

"Yes," I breathed. "*Please.*" I was splayed and begging, and I *loved* it. I wanted to scream and shout, but having to whisper and touch each other without thumping around made me even hornier.

Charlie kissed my mouth, but when I opened for him, he was already licking down my chest. He looked up at me when he reached my dick, watching me as he just barely touched the tip with his tongue, tasting the drops I was leaking. He licked his lips slowly, his eyes glinting as they locked with mine. I shuddered, pretty sure I was about to blow my load.

Then two things happened at once: Charlie swallowed my cock almost all the way, and he slapped his hand over my mouth, smothering my cry. My nostrils flared, the pleasure consuming me. I was on fire, panting wetly against Charlie's palm as he sucked me hard and fast, his other hand wrapped around the base of my shaft.

When he suddenly pulled off, I froze, tearing my gaze from his shiny lips to the door. Was someone there? Were we too loud? Oh my god, was it even *locked?* But before the panic could set in, Charlie was looming over me again, hissing in my ear, "Do you want to fuck my mouth?"

I couldn't stifle my moan as I nodded. I let Charlie push and prod me until our positions were reversed and he was on his back. He tugged on my thighs until I straddled his head. My chest heaved as I leaned over and fed my cock between his open lips. The sweet slide of pressure had my eyes rolling back, and I gripped the bed post so I didn't fall over and suffocate him.

I took a few tentative rocks, and Charlie urged me on, gripping my hips. I couldn't really find a rhythm, but it didn't matter because I was so close. Grunting, I fucked deeply into his mouth, his lips stretching around me. He trailed his fingers into the crease of my ass, brushing over my hole, and a tremor rocked me.

My orgasm flared white hot as I shot into Charlie's mouth. He coughed and sputtered, and I pulled out, splashing the last pulses over his face. He closed his eyes, his mouth wide open and head back. My cum was white against his face in the moonlight, and I wished I could take a picture of how beautiful he looked. Instead, I leaned over and licked it up, which made him groan and kiss me hard.

I reached into his PJs for his cock, and it only took a few tugs before he came, making a heck of a mess. Panting, I flopped down, half on top of him with my face in his neck. Charlie wrapped his arms slowly around me and kissed my head.

"I know you're Jewish, but merry Christmas. Thank you for getting me home."

"After that, I'm thinking of converting. Pretty sure I saw Jesus."

We laughed too loudly, and then shushed each other and held on for a long time after.

Charlie

"Mrs. Yates, that was amazing." Sitting across from me at the dining table, Gavin patted his stomach. "I'm stuffed. With stuffing."

I smiled at his little joke, and Ava poked me in the side, giggling. I tried to tickle under her arm, but she squirmed away before poking me again. "What?" I asked. Her gaze cut to Gavin and then back to me, but she shook her head, seeming to think better of what she was about to say.

"So glad you enjoyed it, Gavin." Mom sipped her red wine. "It's been wonderful having you."

"Thank you again for serving dinner so early. I'd hate to have missed this."

Mom waved a hand. Her cheeks were rosy, and it was nice seeing her so relaxed. "We always have an early dinner on Christmas. My mother used to have it on the table by four o'clock at the latest." She checked her watch. "Are you all packed up? The Allens should be here soon?"

"Yeah, I'm ready to go." Gavin's smile faded a little. "Charlie, you're sure you don't mind returning the rental car in the morning?"

"No prob. Aunt Wendy, Uncle Fred, and the rest of the fam aren't coming over for second Christmas until the afternoon."

Gavin laughed. "Second Christmas? Is that like the hobbits' second breakfast?"

"Yep. Everyone does their own dinner on Christmas, and every year we get together at someone's house the day after and bring all the leftovers." I grinned. "Plus, we get more presents."

"Sounds pretty awesome," Gavin said.

Dad leaned back in his chair at the end of the table opposite Mom. "Good idea the Allens have, driving up to Stowe on Christmas Day. You should make great time and be ready to hit the slopes first thing in the morning. We should try that one year, Maria. Get the whole family to come along."

"We should," Mom answered, but she didn't sound convinced. "We'll see. Skiing can be dangerous."

Ava tensed up instantly. "I can ski, Mom. Plenty of people do it."

Our mom sighed. "Yes, but people also get hurt. Ski into trees and break bones."

"That's what you said about tobogganing, but everyone does it. Sally McCormack did it yesterday, and she's fine. I'm sick of not doing things!" Ava's voice had become a whine. "You wouldn't even let me join in the snowball fight!"

I put my hand on Ava's back and rubbed a few circles while I popped an eyebrow at Mom. "Seriously? A snowball fight? She'll be fine."

Gripping her wine glass, Mom pressed her lips into a thin line. "You'd be surprised by the things I've seen over the year at the ER." She shared a glance with Dad before exhaling. "But yes, perhaps I'm being a little overprotective."

"We'll have a snowball fight before I go back to school, okay, Bear?" I squeezed her little shoulder.

"Okay." She brightened. "Can Gavin play too?"

"Totally." I really wanted to make a comment about how we could do it tonight if Gavin stayed, but I resisted. "When he gets back from skiing, we'll take him on."

Gavin held up his hands. "Whoa, whoa—two against one? Hardly seems fair."

"Are you chicken?" Ava flapped her elbows and made a clucking sound as we all burst out laughing.

"As you can see, Charlie's a wonderful influence," Dad drily noted.

The tension had thankfully dissipated, and Mom yawned. "I'll be ready for bed before too long. Although I do want to try out my new e-reader." She gave me a grin.

"Hope you like it. Just think—you'll always have hundreds of books in your purse. No more—" I stopped myself in time. "No more running out," I added lamely. I'd been about to say, "no more getting stuck with gross waiting-room magazines," but with Ava in remission, there would be no more hospitals. At least I prayed to the universe that there wouldn't be.

We were finishing helping with the dishes when the doorbell rang. I heard the lilt of Candace's voice as my dad answered, and after Ava and my parents said their hellos and dispersed, it was me, Gavin, and Candace in our little foyer. Not awkward at all.

I cleared my throat. "Um, hi. Merry Christmas."

She smiled tentatively. She really was a pretty girl, all blonde waves and white teeth. "Thank you, Charlie. You too." She wore a matching blue and pink scarf/hat/gloves set, and had basically just walked out of a Gap holiday ad.

Might as well just rip the Band-Aid off, right? "I'm sorry for what I said to you that day in the pizza place. It was awful and wrong, and I'm really, really sorry."

Candace blinked. "Oh. Well, apology accepted." She glanced at Gavin. "If Gav can forgive and forget, so can I."

It was asinine that jealousy drilled a shiv into me because she called him "Gav," but there it was all the same. She'd had him for four long years, and now she was taking him again. "Cool. Thanks." I wanted to sling my arm around him and stake my claim. I'd have whipped it out and peed on his leg if I thought it would help. "So you'll be back the thirtieth? But you have to see your folks and stuff, right? I guess I'll just see you whenever." I tried for casual and probably failed wildly.

Gavin stared at me, opening and closing his mouth a few times. Finally, he said, "Oh."

Shit. What did that mean? As I scrambled to think of what to say, Candace backed out. "I'll wait for you in the car. Later, Charlie!" She waved and made her escape, closing the front door behind her. Now Gavin and I were left staring at each other.

The roar of a football game echoed from the den beyond the kitchen. Words whipped through my head like a hurricane, and finally I went for a shrug that probably looked like a seizure. "I mean, assuming you want to see me again." He did, right? I'd felt so close to him, but talking about it made it all suddenly weird and awkward.

"Is that...do you want to see *me* again?"

Yes, yes, yes! But I deflected, because I suck. "Is that what you want? If this was just a hookup, that's cool." *If by "cool," you mean the worst thing ever.*

"I don't think so." He dropped his chin and stared at the ground.

Wait, what? "You don't think so...like, you don't want to see me again?"

He jerked up his head. "No. I don't think it's cool if it was just a hookup." Raising his hands, he said, "Let's start this again, and stop talking circles around it." Gavin's shoulders rose as he inhaled and exhaled deeply. "I don't want this to only be a hookup. I want to see you again as soon as I can. I'm really tempted to bail on skiing, but it would be way too rude."

"Oh." I smiled so hard my face hurt. "Okay. That's awesome. I want to see you again too. I want to see you all the time, basically."

"Yeah?" He ducked his head and smiled sweetly. "Good. I want that too."

"You didn't tell your dad you were even with me on the trip, so I thought maybe…" Crap. Didn't mean to actually say that out loud. I hitched my shoulder spastically. "I caught a little of your call when I got out of the shower yesterday. I wasn't trying to eavesdrop. It was just, you know, thin walls. Sorry."

His face creased. "No, I'm sorry. It really wasn't about you. I have to tell them about me first. But I knew if my dad found out you were with me, he'd probably freak, and we had to get back on the road. It just wasn't the right time."

"I get that. I do. But you're going to tell them soon? About you? And about me…about *us*? There's an us, right?"

"There's totally an us. A hundred percent." After glancing down the hall, he stepped close, nuzzling my cheek and breathing me in. "I hate leaving you right now. But I'll text and—" He stood up straighter, blinking. "Crap. I don't actually have your number." He pulled out his phone, and I rattled off the digits. "Let me just call you, and then you can add me."

My phone buzzed, and my heart skipped as I took it out of my pocket and looked at the picture of Gavin on the screen. He was about to say something else, but his jaw snapped shut.

"What…is that…?"

We both stared at fourteen-year-old Gavin, all bony shoulders and dimpled grin, the auburn in his hair just coming out as it dried. The sun peeked through the willow tree shadowing the side of the pond.

The screen went dark as the call hit my voicemail. I cleared my throat. "I guess I never deleted your contact."

His nostrils flared slightly as his Adam's apple bobbed. Then he pulled me close and just held me against him, leaning down to press his face into my neck. He murmured something I couldn't make out.

When he straightened up, he kissed me gently. The tremor that flowed through me was buttery warm.

"I need a picture." Gavin brushed a hand over my hair.

"I'll send you one while you're skiing. I'll send you a bunch. You can pick."

"Mmm. Intriguing. Will you be wearing pants in any of them?"

"Unlikely."

Gavin grinned, a flare of light, quickly dimming. "Anyway. I'm coming back New Year's Eve, and they'll be home. I'm going to tell them everything."

I rubbed his sides. "You must be worried about what they'll say."

He tried to smile. "Just a little. I'm going to do it, though. I've been keeping this all inside for so long. I can't do it anymore. No matter what happens, I have to be honest. I have to be…real. You know what I mean? I'm going to tell them. I am." He glanced down the hall. "Were your parents always cool with it?"

"Yeah. My mom said she'd already guessed, and when I told them, Ava was in the hospital after the diagnosis." I grimaced. "I guess I picked a hell of a time, but I felt like I was lying to them, and I hated it. But they said they were really glad I told them. I think Ava being sick put shit in perspective."

"I'm so glad she's better. She's such an awesome kid, Charlie. You're really lucky."

I *was* really lucky, and I had to swallow hard over the lump in my throat as I nodded.

"I should go. I'll see you in five days. Actually, more like four days and twenty-three hours. Not that I'm counting."

I pressed our lips together, and we wrapped our arms around each other. I wanted to push him up against the door and kiss him for days. "Four days, twenty-two hours, and fifty-nine minutes," I muttered.

With a final kiss and wave, he was gone, and I locked the door, turning to lean against it as I listened to the Allens' car reverse and drive off down the street.

"You looove him."

I twisted my neck to see Ava at the top of the dark stairs, where she'd apparently been eavesdropping. I couldn't even be mad, though. I tried to hide my smile. "Why do you think that?"

Ava's grin lit up her whole face as she clambered halfway down and parked herself. "You totally do. I can tell. You can't get that look off your face."

"What look?" But I laughed, because I knew I had to have the goofiest smile.

"*That* one. Like you're about to float away on a fluffy cloud of looove." She giggled. "He has the same look."

That made my heart jump. "Yeah?"

"Definitely. He looks like he wants to make kissy faces at you all the time."

My fluffy cloud of looove darkened a bit as doubts hissed like rain. *What if he changes his mind? What if his parents freak and he runs back into the closet? Back to Candace? What if he decides he doesn't like me after all? He got by without me before.*

"What's wrong?"

I blinked back to attention to find Ava watching me with her little brow furrowed. "Nothing. I just need to shake off my doubts." I gave my limbs a spastic shimmy. "Want to help?"

Clapping with such joy it made my heart swell, she bounded down the stairs. We shook ourselves like crazed dogs fresh out of the pond, hopping around until we collapsed by the Christmas tree in the den in a heap of laughter. Dad was glued to the game, and Mom glanced up from her e-reader to ask if I'd spiked the eggnog.

Best Christmas ever.

Nine

Gavin

December 30th

From the foot of my driveway, I could see my dad was working in the garage. The gray day was waning quickly, and light shone around the brown rectangle of the garage door. I waved to Candace and her parents as they drove away with a cheery honk, then squinted down the street. The Yates lived ten houses away near the end of the block, and I wasn't sure if the lights were on.

The garage door whirred open, disappearing upwards. My dad appeared in jeans and a winter jacket, wiping his hands on a rag and smiling hard, wrinkles fanning out from his eyes and mouth. It made me ache. "There's my boy! Did you have fun?" He pulled me into a hug, and I clung to him. He smelled like grease and coffee and *Dad*.

"Hey," I mumbled.

He stepped back and glanced down the street. "I was hoping to say hi to Candace and her folks. Did you have fun on the slopes?"

"Yeah. They had to get going, sorry." A bald-faced lie. They'd wanted to say hi too, but I needed to have this conversation with my dad before the pressure in my chest splintered my ribs. I tried to smile. "Looks like you had fun on the beach. Nice tan."

"Not bad, huh?" His teeth looked whiter than usual. He was tall like me, and we resembled each other in the face, although his hair was black. I'd gotten my auburn brown from my mom. Dad's smile faded. "Everything okay? Come on inside—we're letting out the heat."

I followed into the garage, dragging my little suitcase over hard bumps of snow still scattered across the asphalt. I pressed the big button to close the door after me, and it hummed its way back down as I peered around at the familiar space. It was a double garage, and Mom's Audi was parked on the left beside the work area. Dad had a space heater plugged in near his workbench. The snowblower sat on the floor with its outer shell removed and its guts exposed.

Dad scratched his head. "This darn thing isn't quite getting the job done. Want to shine that flashlight in there?"

It was so tempting to pick up the flashlight and pretend nothing was wrong. It would be so easy. Smile and nod and laugh at the right times, just like I had for the past four years.

"Gav?" Dad straightened up from where he'd bent over the snowblower. "What's up?"

I took off my Little America mitts and fiddled with them. "I didn't mention it to you before, but I ended up driving home with someone from high school. It was a coincidence—we were both trying to rent a car."

He smiled tentatively. "Yeah?"

I didn't let myself look away. "It was Charlie Yates."

Dad's flinch was like a slap to my face. He tried to smile. "Oh, from down the street?"

"You know exactly who he is, Dad. He's the boy I kissed when I was fourteen. The boy I didn't talk to again after I told you what happened. The boy I loved all these years, even when I tried to hate him."

114

His face creased. "Gavin… I don't know what you want me to say."

"I want you to say it's okay! I want you to say you love me just the way I am, and that I'm the same person, and this doesn't change anything." My breath caught in my throat. "That's what I wanted you to say four years ago. I was so scared, Dad. And I needed you to say it was okay. I hid for four years and lied to myself, and to everyone else. I lied to Candace. I'm lucky she's still my friend. And it was all because I was afraid you wouldn't love me anymore."

Tears sprang to his eyes. "Of course I love you. How could you think I wouldn't? If you'd…I…"

"If I'd what, Dad? What was I supposed to do? You told me I was confused. You sounded so sure of it. I thought you had to be right. I *wanted* you to be right, because clearly if I were gay, it was something to be ashamed of."

"No." He spoke firmly. "I never said that."

"You told me not to tell Mom!" My cry filled the garage, and we stared at each other in the ensuing silence. The hurt scraped through me, hollowing out another chunk of my heart. "If it wasn't something to be ashamed of, why did you say that? What else was I supposed to think? I came to you because I trusted you. Because I needed your help."

Warm air wafted over me, and I turned to find my mom in the door leading into the house. She wore her slippers, slacks, and her fancy green cashmere sweater, which meant she'd cooked a dinner she was proud of. With her standing at the top of the three steps, we were the same height for once. "He told you not to tell Mom what?"

"Andrea, it's okay. Go back inside, and we'll be in soon." Dad put on a smile and wiped his hands with a rag. "Just finishing up in here."

"I'm gay, Mom." The words hung there, the space heater buzzing and the distant TV murmuring.

Mom stared between me and my father. "What?"

"You heard me. I'm gay."

She made a little snorting sound as she shook her head. "What? Gavin, that's ridiculous. Is this a joke?"

"Andrea, let me talk to Gavin, and—"

"No, Dad. You both need to hear this. I've hid this for so long. I'm gay. I always have been. I always will be. This is how I was born."

"But how can that be?" Mom stared at me incredulously. "No, honey. You and Candace. You love her."

"I do. But not like that."

"I don't understand. You and Candace were so happy. Did something happen at college? I know San Francisco is liberal-minded and that can confuse—"

"I've always been gay. It's not new."

She wrapped her arms around her stomach and took a step back, staring at my father. "I don't understand."

Dad sighed. "Gavin, are you sure that you're not…" He waved his hand around.

"No, Dad. I'm not confused. I wasn't then, and I'm not now. It's not a phase. It's forever. It's the way I was born."

"So you're saying…" Mom blinked owlishly. "But I never thought… I'm your mother. I should have known." She pressed her hand to her mouth. "I should have known!"

I wanted to agree, but I couldn't bear to hurt her any worse. "It's not your fault I never told you."

Tears slipped down her cheeks. "But Gavin…"

"I know it's not what you want to hear, Mom."

She clutched her hands together. "There are so many things you'll miss out on."

"Maybe some things will be different, but—"

"*Some* things?" She shook her head. "What about children? *My* grandchildren?"

"Huh? What about them?" I almost wanted to laugh, it was so surreal. "I'm eighteen. I'm not having kids for years."

She pressed her lips together. "But if you're gay, then…"

I took a deep breath, trying to stay in control. "Gay people can have kids, Mom."

"Oh, Gavin. No. It's just not right! Children need a mother and father."

"Children need parents who love them the way they are!" My shout was swallowed by the dull concrete.

"Darling, if you make this choice, think of all the obstacles you'll face! Jake, talk to him." She spun to face Dad. "You don't want this for him any more than I do."

Dad shook his head. "It's not a choice. Is it, Gavin?"

My eyes burned, but I managed to speak without sobbing. "It really isn't. I tried to choose. When Dad told me I was confused, I wanted to believe him. I didn't want to let you both down."

"Oh, Gavin. I'm sorry." Dad ran his hand over his face. "God. I'm so sorry."

Mom glared daggers at him. "When exactly did this conversation take place?"

"The summer we moved here," I answered. "Right before school started. I was friends with Charlie Yates that summer. I didn't know anyone else, and we spent hours together every day. Remember?"

"I remember. He was a nice boy. I assumed you drifted apart. I never really thought much about it."

"Labor Day weekend, we…we kissed. Made out." I waited to see if she'd flinch or grimace or maybe puke, yet she only watched me steadily. "Then we went to a party and I met Candace. She liked me, but I didn't like her the way I did Charlie. I told Dad everything, and he said I was confused. He said I wasn't gay."

I sniffed loudly, swiping at the tears dripping down my face before going on. "But I knew I was. I knew it. I'd had crushes on other boys, even though I'd never admitted it to myself. But I was afraid, so I tried to be straight. I dated Candace, and I never even talked to Charlie again. It was terrible, what I did. They both deserved better. I hurt them so much."

"It wasn't your fault," Dad said.

"Of course it was! Even if it was your fault too, in the end it was my choice. I thought if I was strong enough, I could do it. I could be who you wanted me to be."

Mom pressed her hand to her chest. "Oh, darling."

"I can't, though." I looked back and forth between them. "I'm gay, and I won't pretend anymore. Charlie hated me for the way I turned my back on him, but he forgave me. We drove home together, and we became friends again. More than friends."

"You and Charlie?" She blinked, and I could practically see the wheels turning in her head as she tried to process it.

"We had sex," I blurted. "I'm gay. Like, officially." My face must have been beet red, but I needed to lay it all out on the table.

The shrill ring of my dad's cell phone on the workbench made us all jump. Dad grabbed it and flicked the button for the ringer. A swell of fake sitcom laughter from the TV inside filled the silence.

Mom looked at me with such sorrow that I wanted to turn away. "I don't know what to say, Gavin. You're my son, and I love you more than anything in this world. But this isn't what I want for you. This isn't... I don't know what to make of it. I had dreams for you. Dreams of how your life would be. This...this will ruin everything for you, honey." Fresh tears tracked down her cheeks. "Life will be so hard. You can't want this. Not truly."

"I think—" Dad's voice was hoarse, and he cleared his throat. "I think we just need some time to get used to it."

Quietly, I said, "You've had four years, Dad."

He hung his head, and Mom kept crying. I couldn't be there anymore. I backed up and jammed my finger against the button for the garage door. It lurched up with a mechanical jolt. "I'm going to Charlie's. I'll talk to you later."

Salt crunched under my boots as I ran down the block. Christmas lights shone from the houses I passed, blurs of color as I tried to stop crying. On the Yates' driveway, I stood behind their

SUV and breathed in and out for a few minutes. I was a snotty mess, and I needed to get in control before—

"Gavin?" Charlie's voice rang out in the night. "Is that you?"

He'd shoved his feet into boots, and was only wearing a sweater and jeans as he came down the walkway to the front door, squinting. I wiped my face and attempted a smile, which was clearly unsuccessful given the way Charlie's eyes widened as he rushed forward to wrap his arms around me.

"What happened? Gav?" I could only stand there sobbing, and he rubbed my back. "Shh. It's okay. I'm here."

And he was. God, Charlie was there, and warmth flowed through me, soothing all the jagged edges. "Thank you."

He shushed me some more, and even though I was bigger than him, I felt so safe in his arms. It was below freezing, but he held me there on his driveway for what seemed like hours, until I was able to stand up straight and form complete sentences. I told him what happened, and he gripped my hands.

"They'll come around," he insisted. "I know they will."

"You don't know that for sure. I want to think so, but…"

"I do know it, because you're too good for them not to. They're going to process, and work out their shit, and in the end, it'll be okay. It will. They're not bad people. I'm not saying I don't want to march over there and scream at them, because I do. Like, a lot. For an hour at least. But they're not bad. They love you. It'll be okay. They won't be able to handle losing you. Trust me."

I sniffed a few times, swallowing some snot. "I don't deserve you."

He rolled his eyes. "Get off the cross. Someone needs the wood."

The laughter that ripped out of me was so unexpected and *wonderful*. "I guess that's one way to put it."

"It's not like I haven't made my fair share of dick moves in my lifetime. You're not perfect. I'm sure as hell not. No one is."

"God, I love you." The words flowed out so naturally that I didn't even realize I'd said them until Charlie's jaw dropped. "I mean…" Squaring my shoulders, I took a deep breath. "Actually, that's exactly what I mean. I love you, Charlie. All these years, I watched you from a distance, and I loved you. And I was a coward. You were hurting and scared and dealing with a nightmare, and I didn't even have the guts to be your friend. I know it's only been— what, barely two weeks since we've even *spoken* again, and I don't expect—"

He pressed his cold finger over my lips. "I love you too. Even when I told myself I hated you, I still loved you. It was always you, Gavin." With trembling hands, he held my face and pressed kisses to my forehead, chin, both cheeks, and the tip of my nose, his lips a whisper against my skin. "Always will be."

I was going to cry again, so I kissed him instead and let go of the past, taking hold of joy with both hands.

Charlie

It wasn't quite midnight when I edged open the door to the guest room, scratching the wood softly with my blunt nails. As I suspected, Gavin was wide awake. I tiptoed to the bed and pressed a kiss to his lips.

"Charlie, I'm not really…is it okay if we don't…" He motioned his hand between us.

I brushed back his thick hair. "This isn't a booty call. Just wanted to check up on you."

"Oh." With a sweet smile dawning on his face, he lifted the duvet. I slipped in, cuddling up close with our feet tangled. On our sides facing each other, I could make out his expression in the glow from the digital clock. Reaching up, I traced my finger along his eyebrows.

"I know it's hard," I murmured. "They really will come around."

"It wasn't hard for you."

"Not really. They said all the right stuff. Supported me and made sure I knew it. It still felt like things had changed, though. Like they were looking at me with new eyes."

"In what way?"

I slid my hands up under his tee so I could play with his chest hair. I'd meant it when I said this wasn't a booty call, but I wanted to touch him all the time now that I could. "Like, we'd be watching a ball game after being at the hospital all day, and I'd say something about a player. You know—'Ramirez has a hell of an arm' or whatever. And they'd look at me, and then look at the TV like they were wondering if I wanted to bone the guy. It was just awkward at first."

"But not anymore."

"Nope. With Ava being sick, they really didn't have time to think about me."

His brow creasing, Gavin rubbed his hand over my hip. "I'm sorry."

"No, don't be. I shouldn't—I'm making it sound like I was hard done by. Of course they still thought about me. Still loved me. They always made sure I knew that. But in a weird way, it took the pressure off. If I wanted to fuck a baseball player, they were like, Sure, great, whatever."

"I see what you mean." He rested his hand on my hip, sneaking under my pajama bottoms to rub circles with his thumb.

"I met Tim and they were totally cool with it. I was definitely lucky in that regard."

Gavin's lip curled, his hand stilling. "Right. *Tim.*"

As it hit me, I tried to choke down the burst of laughter. "Dude, are you jealous?"

He seemed about to deny it, but then shrugged. "Totally. I saw him pick you up from school once, and I wanted to puke."

"Now you know how I felt seeing you with Candace every damn day."

Suddenly, there was a weird tension in the air, both of us still touching each other but not moving.

"That must have sucked so much," he whispered.

"Yeah. But it's over now." I splayed my hands on his chest, rubbing his nipples with my thumbs.

Gavin rubbed our noses together. "I love touching you." His hand dipped over my ass cheek, his fingers teasing my crease.

"I love you touching me too." I kissed his smile away, exploring his mouth, my hands roaming down over his belly to tease the trail of hair leading to his groin.

"I thought this wasn't a booty call," he murmured against my lips.

With—if I do say so myself—an impressive amount of intestinal fortitude, I pulled back. His hand stilled on my ass. "It's not. We can just talk." I brushed my knuckles over his cheek. "I know you're hurting."

"I don't really have anything else to say. Either they'll accept me or they won't. Right now I just…I'd rather you kissed it better."

So I did.

We kissed and kissed, sweet and dirty and wet, and before long our clothes were tossed away. I honestly could have just kissed him all night and rubbed off against his stomach. He rolled on top of me, hard and heavy, and I spread my legs for him.

"I missed you so much the last few days," he muttered. "*Years.*"

My heart clenched, and I took his face in my hands, slowing things down with a gentle kiss. I hooked my leg over his, rubbing steadily. "Years," I agreed. "Now we get to make up for lost time. And we know what we're doing, which makes it more fun."

His puff of embarrassed laughter warmed my face. "*You* know what you're doing."

"You're an extremely quick study. Trust me."

"I dreamed of this so many nights. I can't believe we're really here." He kissed my cheek, making my insides go all gooey even as we rocked our hips together, getting harder and harder.

"Tell me what else you dreamed of."

He blinked. "I dunno. Stuff. I told you most of it. You know, with the thing."

"Mmm." Sliding my hand over his back, I traced his hole with my fingertip. "What thing was that again?"

"*Charlie.*"

I swore I could *feel* the heat of his blush. "You mean when you fucked yourself with the dildo and imagined it was my cock?"

"Yes," he whispered, rocking our dicks together deliciously.

Biting back a gasp, I asked, "What else did you fantasize about?"

"That's all. Just stuff." He kissed me hard, cutting off my reply.

I let him kiss me for a minute, our tongues stroking and my cock leaking. Then I broke away. "What is it? There's something you don't want to tell me."

He ducked his head to suck on my collar bone. Threading my fingers through his hair, I caressed him. "You can tell me anything. You know that, don't you? Do you think it's too weird or something?"

Lifting his head only an inch or so, Gavin sighed against my skin. "It's kind of…out there." His voice was muffled against my neck. "I've seen it in porn, but I don't know if, you know. If normal people who aren't porn stars do it."

"Well now you *have* to tell me, or I'll be imagining all sorts of freaky shit."

His laughter was a wet huff. He kept his head down. "It's rimming, okay?"

My brain exploded.

After a moment, he asked, "Is that weird?"

Somehow I managed to talk. "If by 'weird,' you mean super hot, then sure." My dick throbbed, and I thrust up against him.

Gavin's head shot up. "Really? Have you…?"

"Uh-uh. It's never come up, so to speak."

"But you'd want to?" His expression was so eager he looked like a puppy. A puppy thrusting his hard cock against me.

123

"You showered before bed, right?"

As he nodded, I was already urging him off me and onto his stomach. He spread his legs so hungrily it made my balls tighten. I kneeled behind him. "You want it? You want me to eat your ass?" Maybe I sounded like a cheesy porno, but with Gavin I loved saying it out loud.

He actually whimpered, nodding vigorously. We had to be quiet, and I couldn't wait until I had him in bed again without my family down the hall. I pushed those thoughts away and spread his ass cheeks. "You have to be quiet, okay?"

He nodded again, and I eyed his pucker. I couldn't see much in the murky night, so I figured what the hell. Leaning over, I opened him and buried my face in his ass, licking around his hole. Gavin jerked, his shout muffled in the mattress. So far, so good. I licked again, sweeping my tongue along his crease.

As Gavin trembled and thrust his ass up for more, I held him still and tried to lick inside him. I'm not sure what I was expecting it to taste like, but aside from a bit of salty tang from us getting sweaty grinding each other, it didn't really taste different from the rest of him.

I didn't really know what I was doing, but he seemed to like it. Actually, he seemed to love it, his muffled moans making me so hot I had to stretch out and hump the mattress while I ate him.

Gavin shook all over, and with one hand, I fondled his balls while I spit into his hole and tried to lick deeper. Maybe it was weird, and maybe 'normal people'—whoever the hell they were—didn't do this, but I loved having my face in his ass.

I thought about how it would feel to have him do it to me, and I moaned against his flesh. With a mighty tremble, he came, groaning into the sheets. I reached down for my dick and only needed a few tugs before I joined him, the pleasure sweeping through me. I gasped against his ass.

Resting my cheek on his cheek—which made me chuckle to myself—I caught my breath. I rubbed the back of his thigh lazily, my eyes drifting shut. It would have been heaven to fall asleep right then, using Gavin's ass as a pillow.

"I have to go back to my own room," I murmured. I still didn't move, though, trailing my fingers up and down his leg.

"Mmm."

After another minute, I roused myself, pushing up over him and kissing my way up his spine. "Did you like it?"

"Is that a trick question?" After a moment, he asked, "Did you?"

Smiling, I nuzzled the back of his neck, holding myself up on my hands. "I loved it."

"I'm glad we could...do something new for you."

His face was turned to the side, and I stretched out beside him so we could kiss again. I'd never get tired of kissing him. "It's all new," I mumbled.

Gavin frowned, inching back and rolling onto his hip to fully face me. "But you did stuff before."

I brushed my palm over his mussed hair. "That was nothing compared to this. It's different with you." Leaning in, I pressed our lips together. "It's different when you're in love."

He wrapped his arms around me, squeezing so tightly for a moment that I couldn't breathe.

Breathing was overrated.

Ten

Charlie

December 31ˢᵗ

"Do you want to have that snowball fight?"

Gavin's eyes were puffy, but he smiled gamely at Ava from beside me on the couch in the den. "Always."

She clapped and grinned at me. "He got the right answer!"

"Of course he did. He got into Stanford, after all. Now go pee before you put your snowsuit on." Ava raced off, and I gave Gavin a wink. "That's our little joke. Whenever someone asks you if you want to do something fun, the answer is 'always,' no matter what. But are you sure you're up for it?"

He'd been very firm that he didn't want to talk about it, and we'd spent the day watching movies and playing video games and generally being couch potatoes. Gavin had checked his phone a million times, and I'd barely resisted the urge to march down the street and order his parents to yank their heads out of their asses.

"Absolutely! I'm fine, Charlie. I'm good." He popped another one of my mom's famous meatballs into his mouth.

126

"Mmm-hmm. So you keep saying. We can go over there, you know. Talk to them some more. My parents can help. They said they would."

"No, it's New Year's Eve. Your parents probably haven't had a date night in ages. It wouldn't be fair." He spun a toothpick between his fingers, watching it intently. "They have to talk to me sooner or later. Come on, we promised Ava."

Mom and Dad came downstairs as we were gearing up. I whistled. "You clean up pretty well."

Mom slapped my shoulder and did a little spin, her crimson dress flaring around her knees. "Not bad for an old broad, huh?"

"You look beautiful, Mrs. Yates," Gavin said.

Dad pulled his overcoat over his fancy suit and held out Mom's coat. "All right, you've got the numbers, Charlie?"

I rolled my eyes. "The National Guard's on standby. Go! Have fun!" I put a giggling Ava in a playful headlock. "I'll try to keep her in one piece."

Mom ignored me and addressed Gavin. "Keep an eye on them." Then she held out her arms to Ava. "I'll see you soon, all right?" She hugged Ava tightly and kissed her head. "If you need anything—"

"*Moooom.* I'm fine." Ava let go of Mom and finished zipping up her snowsuit. "Charlie always takes good care of me. And Gavin's here to take care of him."

Mom and Dad looked at each other, lingering on the threshold. I knew this was the first time they'd left Ava in years—like, literally *years*, especially for my mom. I regarded them seriously. "Go have a nice dinner. I'll call if anything happens."

They nodded, and Mom kissed my cheek and then swiped at the lipstick mark with her thumb. We stood in the doorway and waved as they drove away, and then Ava thumped her wool-clad hands together. "Let's do this."

It had been snowing off and on all day, and as we headed to the park a couple blocks away, Ava ran ahead, delighting in making fresh tracks in the unbroken swathes of white. Then she raced back and lifted her arms to me.

"Piggy!"

I pretended to think about it. "Gosh, I dunno. You're awfully big now, Bear."

She roared and tugged me down so she could clamber onto my back. The knees of my jeans got soaked in the snow, but I didn't care as I took off. She really was much heavier now, and it felt so damn good when I had to stop and readjust my grip to hoist her higher.

I glanced back at Gavin, who trotted behind us with a huge smile as we entered the park. Fluffy flakes drifted down in the calm breeze, catching in Gavin's thick hair. Christmas lights twinkled all around, the trees in the park decorated to the hilt by the neighborhood committee.

The trees and bushes beyond the playground offered excellent hiding places, and we discovered a few boys had had the same idea. Ava apparently knew them from school, and they chattered about their Christmas gifts.

I hung back and watched, grinning. When Gavin gave me a quizzical look, I leaned in and murmured, "It's just great seeing Ava do normal things. It was really hard for her being in and out of the hospital and missing so much school."

"Okay, so it's us against you two," Ava announced, marching over to me and Gavin with the two boys in tow.

"Three against two? Gavin, I feel like we've been set up here."

Ava just laughed. "You're both big, so it's totally fair. We're going over there, and you go here."

"So what are the r—" A snowball whacked me straight in the face, and I sputtered as Gavin tugged my arm. We ducked behind some shrubs.

He laughed. "Apparently there are no rules."

"They will rue the day!" I pronounced dramatically. We went to work on a cache of snowballs, firing them strategically. I popped up to launch one, and got another direct hit, the snowball smashing on my nose. I brushed off the snow and clenched my jaw. "I'm going to bean that little jerk with an ice ball if he doesn't watch it."

"Charlie!" Gavin gave me an exasperated smile. "He's a kid!"

"Wait, so I shouldn't attempt to give him a traumatic brain injury?" I sighed heavily. "I guess I'll resist, just this once. But only because you're here, Saint Gavin."

Chuckling, he shook his head. "Okay, fair enough. But I'll have you know that your sarcasm can be incredibly convincing."

"Only for those as earnest as you, babe." Gavin ducked a snowball that whizzed by overhead, and he was positively beaming when he sat back up. I couldn't hide my own smile. "You like it when I call you that?"

Blushing, he packed snow in his gloves and nodded. "It's nice."

It *was* pretty freaking nice, wasn't it? I tried to think of a witty remark, but all I could do was steal a kiss. He leaned into me, all warm breath and sweet lips…

I emitted an extremely manly combination gasp/screech at the icy wetness on my neck as the sly bastard shoved a handful of snow down the back of my shirt. I shot to my feet and hopped around, stretching back to scoop out as much as I could as Gavin howled.

Ava and the boys naturally took this opportunity to blast me with more snowballs, and finally I just stood there and took it as missiles smacked into me from all directions. Laughter echoed through the trees as I wiped the snow from my sodden face with my gloves.

I extended an accusing finger toward Gavin crouched on the ground. "It's always the quiet ones! And don't think you're off the hook, little sister! I'll have my revenge!" I shook my fist.

Of course it ended with all of them ganging up on me, and I collapsed in the snow and let them have at it. I did manage to tumble Gavin off his feet, and our jeans and jackets were soaked by the time we made it home, shivering. Man, I wanted to have a long, hot shower with him, but instead we were responsible and changed into dry clothes before ordering pizza and settling down in the den with Ava.

Soon, Ava's head bobbed onto my shoulder, and she jerked upright. "I'm still awake!"

Chuckling, I patted her hip, my arm wrapped around her. I was in the middle of the couch with Gavin on my left and Ava on my right, watching the show from Times Square with pizza stuffing our bellies and junk food spread before us on the coffee table.

Maybe I should have preferred to be at some wild party on New Year's Eve, but I was exactly where I wanted to be. Mom and Dad had texted a photo from the fancy restaurant where they were having dinner, and their smiles glowed. "Bear, maybe it's time for bed."

She shook her head vehemently, her new little curls flying. "It's not midnight. I have to stay up for the ball. Mom and Dad said I could."

"I know, but you're pooped. Still two hours to go."

She bit her thumbnail. "Maybe I'll have a nap. Only if you promise to wake me before twelve. Please? I really want to stay up."

"Okay. Why is it so important? The new year will still happen." I ran my palm over her head.

"Because I didn't think I'd get to see next year. So I want to be awake for it." She answered so nonchalantly, like life and death was something she dealt with every day—probably because it was.

My throat tightened, and Gavin blinked rapidly. I kissed the top of Ava's head. "I'll make sure you see it, Bear. Promise."

She was asleep almost in an instant, and Gavin held my hand while we watched Ryan Seacrest interview Taylor Swift, who had to be freezing in a strapless dress.

Gavin cleared his throat. "I have a confession."

My heart skipped. "Um, okay." I peeked down at Ava curled against me, but she was out.

"I like Taylor Swift. I like her new song, and I like the whole album, actually." His declaration was punctuated by Taylor launching into said new song on TV. She was clearly singing live, and she

130

sounded pretty great. And damn it, that song was catchy and fun, just like the shake song.

"I like it too," I mumbled.

"Are you just saying that?"

"Nope." I sighed. "I know it's hard to believe, what with my super cool street cred and all."

Gavin laughed. "It's just…at school when you'd have your earbuds in all the time, scowling, I imagined you listening to, I dunno. Scandinavian death metal or something."

"Oh, I do have a huge Scandinavian death metal playlist. Have you heard of Bloody Fjords? Good stuff. Evocative. And loud. Look, I'm not saying I love all of T-Swift's catalog, but you'd have to be cold and dead inside—much like Bloody Fjords—not to tap your toes to this one. A good song is a good song. I'm not going to be a snob about it."

"Good to know." Gavin's dimples creased his face. "Another confession: If we ever drive across the country again, I want to stop and see the big ball of twine, or wax, or the huge banana or whatever."

"Because Little America wasn't cheesy Americana enough for you?" I grinned back at him.

"Nope. I need more."

"Bring it on. I can take it." The idea struck me so hard I almost jumped up off the couch. "Why don't we rent a car again and drive back? Postpone our flights for next time? We don't have classes until the second week of January. If we leave in a couple of days, we'll have time."

"Are you serious? Yes. Let's do it. This time without a flat tire and fighting."

I rolled my eyes. "You just totally jinxed us, dude. Knock on wood." I reached up and gave his head a sharp rap.

The faint knock on the front door came a moment later, and Gavin and I stared at each other, puzzled. I eased out from under Ava, who barely stirred as I settled her on the cushions. I left the den and hurried around the kitchen and down the hall, wondering if the pizza guy accidentally came back. Not that I could fit even another slice in my belly.

I probably should have expected to find the Bloombergs standing there in their coats and scarves with worn faces and dark circles under their eyes. But I stared at them with my mouth agape for at least a few seconds before I got it together enough to invite them inside.

They removed their boots, and I awkwardly took their coats before ushering them into the front room, which we hardly ever used. It had that stiff, sitting room quality. The furniture was classic and pristine, and the Bloombergs perched on the couch while I went to get drinks and their son. They were dressed in button-up shirts and slacks—not fancy, but not lounge wear either. I wondered if they'd had plans tonight that they canceled.

Gavin glanced up with a frown when I came back into the den. I whispered, "It's your parents," and his eyes widened.

I hung back in the kitchen, not sure if I should offer them booze or soda or what. Maybe coffee? Tea? What did grownups drink this late at night at other people's houses? I decided to put together a selection on a little tray. I also decided to take a page from Ava's book and eavesdrop shamelessly.

"Darling, are you all right?" Mrs. Bloomberg's voice sounded raw.

"Yeah. I mean, obviously I'm upset. But I'm okay. Are you?"

"It's been a difficult day," she answered. "Gavin…" She sighed heavily. "Darling, this wasn't how I thought your life would go. I can't say I'm happy about it. But we couldn't let you spend another night thinking that we don't love you the way you are." Her voice thickened with tears. "Because we do. We love you so much."

"Even if I'm gay?" Gavin's voice shook. "Because I am."

"Yes," Mr. Bloomberg answered. "*Yes.* We were up all night arguing and running through all the different scenarios for what your

132

life will be like now. We kept coming back to the same thing. That we love you and support you."

"You really do?"

I strained to hear Mr. Bloomberg's low response. "Son, I…" He cleared his throat, speaking more confidently. "I should have said it four years ago. I can't tell you how sorry I am for that. I hope you know that."

"We want the best for you, and you're going to have it." Mrs. Bloomberg's voice cracked. "You're our baby."

I peeked around the corner, and they were standing by the couch, the three of them hugging each other and sniffling. I was getting choked up myself, so I busied myself with the drinks. After a minute, I took the tray in. "Um, can I offer you a drink?"

Wiping her eyes, Mrs. Bloomberg looked at the tray and laughed. "I don't think I've had an orange soda in decades, but sure."

I hadn't even paid attention to the cans I'd pulled out of the fridge. "It was a treat for my sister. I put down the tray on the table and checked the other cans I'd shoved on there. "There's also, um, root beer and cream soda. But I'm pretty sure my mom has Diet Coke. Or water?"

She smiled kindly. "I'm going to live dangerously and have that orange soda. As long as your sister won't mind."

"No, of course not." I poured it into a glass I'd filled with ice and handed it over. After I gave Mr. Bloomberg a root beer, we all sat, the three of them on the couch and me in a chair. I tried to think of something to say. I felt like Gavin's parents were looking at me and thinking, *He's had sex with our baby.*

"I went on the internet," Mrs. Bloomberg said.

"I didn't realize you'd heard of it." Gavin smiled at his own joke.

"Har, har. I was dialing up and surfing Netscape when I was pregnant with you, young man. Anyway, your father and I are going to a meeting next week at the library. It's called PFLAG. Parents and friends of lesbians and gays. And I assume transgendered people too." She turned to her husband. "Is that the right term? I think it is. That's what they say on *Orange is the New Black*, isn't it?"

"I think it's right, Mom. And that's really cool about PFLAG. You've been busy."

"Well, I'm not one for sitting idle. If I'm a parent of a gay person, then I'm going to learn all about it."

I had a feeling she was going to learn way more than Gavin might want, but it was pretty awesome.

Gavin said, "Cool. But… Do you still think it's wrong for gay people to have kids? And what about getting married? What do you guys think about that?"

The Bloombergs shared a glance, and Gavin's dad answered. "We don't know. We've always thought…we've always been proponents of traditional marriage. Traditional families."

Ugh. Okay, so that was way less awesome. I had to legit bite my tongue to stop from shouting about how wrong they were for so many reasons. Gavin was ashen, and I wanted to circle the coffee table and take his hand.

Mr. Bloomberg went on. "But when we think of what a wonderful father you'd be…well, it's different when it's you. It changes everything. Makes us think of the world in a whole new way." He rubbed his face. "It's a lot to take in. There are so many things we need to think about. But like your mother said, we couldn't stand the thought of you waking up tomorrow and thinking we don't support you. We do. I'm not saying it's all going to be perfect. But we'll try our best."

Gavin was silent for a few moments, and I itched to know what he was thinking. Finally, he simply said, "Okay. We'll all do our best."

"Will you come home?" Mrs. Bloomberg asked. "We'd really like to talk more with you." She glanced at me. "Not that we don't want to talk to you as well, Charlie. It's just getting late."

"You guys should go to bed," Gavin said. "I'll walk back after midnight. We can talk more in the morning. Maybe you can make pancakes?"

She nodded, wiping away fresh tears. "I have some blueberries in the fridge. Gosh, I haven't made pancakes in a long time."

Gavin shot me a little smile. "I had some the other day. Gave me the taste for them."

We all shuffled into the hallway, and I handed them their coats after they put their boots back on.

Mr. Bloomberg offered his hand. "Thank you for the hospitality, Charlie. I suppose we'll be seeing you soon."

"Yes. Thank you." Gavin's mom shook my hand as well before she and her husband hugged Gavin again.

We stood in the door and watched them walk into the gently falling snow. I closed it and flipped the lock, leaning back. "That was intense."

"Yeah. But I'm so glad they came."

I opened my arms, and we held each other as the new year crept closer.

"Five, four, three, two—one!"

Ava, Gavin and I rattled the dollar store noisemakers and blew out the paper blowy things that unfurled with a *hoot*, jumping up and down on the thick carpet of the den.

"Happy new year!" Ava shouted, doing a pirouette in front of the Christmas tree and laughing gloriously.

"Should old acquaintance be forgot, and never brought to mind?"

Gavin and I looked at each other, and when we kissed, it was so perfect I could hardly stand it. I nuzzled him. "I'm so glad for FOGmaggedon and snowmaggedon, and all the -maggedons."

"Me too." With a grin, Gavin heaved me up and spun me around. "To new beginnings."

"Now me!" Ava held up her arms, and Gavin whirled her into the air while I laughed, my feet still miles off the ground.

Epilogue

Gavin

January 2nd

"So."

"So," Charlie agreed.

I put the key in the ignition of our new rental—a blue Toyota this time. "Ready?"

"I don't know." Charlie took a deep breath and blew it out, his cheeks puffing.

My heart stuttered. "What don't you know about?"

He motioned his hand between us. "About what happens when we get back to San Francisco."

With a dry mouth, I asked, "You don't think we can make it work?"

"You're in Palo Alto. I'm in the city. It's like, an *hour* on the Caltrain. You know what they say about long-distance relationships." He shook his head with mock solemnity.

Relief flowed through me, and although I was really tempted to smack his arm, I put on my best serious expression. "You're right. It might be too much. Guess we shouldn't have wasted all those years we lived on the same block."

Charlie leaned in and kissed me. "We really shouldn't have," he whispered.

"We'll just have to make up for lost time." I slipped my hand under his shirt and caressed his back, his muscles flexing under my fingers. "Wanna start now?"

He kissed me again, his tongue pushing into my mouth and making me moan as he pressed me against the door.

I took that as a resounding yes.

When I turned the key a few minutes later, Charlie plugged in his phone and cued up that Taylor Swift song. We sang along, horribly off-key and not caring even a bit as we drove toward the freeway and our new future, bright as the western sun on the horizon.

The End

About the Author

After writing for years yet never really finding the right inspiration, Keira discovered her voice in gay romance, which has become a passion. She writes contemporary, historical, paranormal and fantasy fiction, and—although she loves delicious angst along the way—Keira firmly believes in happy endings. For as Oscar Wilde once said, "The good ended happily, and the bad unhappily. That is what fiction means."

Exclusive news and giveaways!

Find out more about Keira's books and sign up for her monthly e-newsletter at: **keiraandrews.com**

Made in the USA
Middletown, DE
19 January 2020

83385490R00085